S0-AKN-311

Praise for the First Printing of

THE BINDING By Brenda Barrie

A testimony to the awful power of secrets, the overwhelming burden of history, and the enduring power of love, The Binding is a novel that engages the reader in every way. This book has joined my "you've got to read this" list. It will linger in my imagination for a long, long time.

> **David Haynes**, author of *The Full Matilda* and *Somebody Else's Moma,* Southern Methodist University

In *The Binding*, Brenda Barrie has nailed the psyche of the son of Holocaust survivors. I know, because I am one of them. I see myself (in each one of her major characters).... *The Binding* may be a work of fiction, but it is one of the truest stories I have ever experienced.

> **Charles Adler**, radio talk show host, newspaper columnist, news commentator and analyst for the Global Television Network

The Binding is a thought-provoking book about a second generation still affected by the Holocaust . . . with the pacing of a mystery and the sweetness of a romance . . .Thank goodness we need not say goodbye to (these characters) but meet them again, in far more detail, in Barrie's second novel, *The Rabbi's Husband.*

> **Carol Matas**, author of *Sworn Enemies, Code Name Kris, Lisa's War, The Garden,* and others

THE BINDING

a novel

Second Edition

Gray Matter Imprints, Irvine, California

Also by Brenda Barrie

The Rabbi's Husband (novel, 2011)

Full Speed. Full Stop (poetry, 2003)

THE BINDING

a novel by

Brenda Barrie

For Beverly
My good luck omen
Brenda Barrie
March
2016

THIRD EDITION

Library of Congress Cataloging-in-Publication Data
Barrie, Brenda
The Binding, a novel / Brenda Barrie
    Fiction, Novel, Holocaust, Holocaust Survivors, Children of Holocaust Survivors, Spiritualism, Judaism, Orthodox Judaism, Conservative Judaism, Reform Judaism, Conversion to Judaism.
    ISBN (978-0-9835921-4-3) ISBN-10: 0983592144
    Library of Congress Control Number: xxx
    1. Novel 2. Fiction 3. Holocaust 4. Holocaust Survivors 5. Children of Holocaust Survivors 6. Spiritualism 7. Judaism 8. Orthodox Judaism 9. Conservative Judaism 10. Reform Judaism 11. Conversion to Judaism

The book cover of The Binding was designed by Rena Konheim, based on the stained glass window created by Willet Studios (now Willet Hauser Architectural Glass, Inc.) of Philadelphia, PA, for the First Presbyterian Church in Belmont, NC.

Published by Gray Matter Imprints™, division of Gray Matter Consultants LLC, P.O. Box 50278 Irvine, CA 92619

10 9 8 7 6 5 4 3

Printed in the United States of America

Gray Matter Imprints accepts queries only at:
        Editor
        Gray Matter Imprints
        P.O. Box 50278
        Irvine, CA 92619

For my daughters,
Renata and *Aviva*,
with love

ACKNOWLEDGEMENTS

The Binding originated as my Masters thesis during my studies for an M.A. in Creative Writing at Hamline University in St. Paul, MN. I would like to thank Hamline, and particularly the staff in the Graduate Liberal Studies office, for their extra efforts on my behalf, as I lived in California and Maryland but continued to be a part of the Hamline community.

More than gratitude goes to inspiring teachers at Hamline, gracious, encouraging and accommodating at all times. I must particularly thank the poet Deborah Keenan and novelist David Haynes, now teaching at Southern Methodist University.

Special thanks to the late Pulitzer Prize-winning novelist Carol Shield, a dear friend and book-club fellow from my hometown of Winnipeg, who read my first poems many years ago and helped me get them published. She put forth extra effort to read and comment on early manuscripts of this novel, and is always a model for me.

I have to express gratitude to Rena Konheim of Baltimore, who has been a dear friend since we met in Winnipeg a quarter century ago, has dutifully read every manuscript and offered unlimited help and advice – and created the cover design for this volume and that of *The Rabbi's Husband*.

Thanks and deepest love to my husband Sid Bursten, who knows I can do anything I set my mind to, but who may not know that his support is a crucial ingredient.

It's fashionable to downplay that particular quality known as "Minnesota Nice," but not when you are the recipient. The Sheff family – Virginia, Harold, Harry and Morgan – made me welcome in their home during many summer-school sessions. I appreciated their warmth, the comfort of their beautiful home, the loan of cars, and getting to know their golden retrievers.

When my husband and I moved from Minnesota to California, I was fortunate to meet one of the best writing teachers of our time, Louella Nelson, and to become part of her Friday afternoon writing class along with Alexis, Diane, Deborah, Erica, Judy and Janice. Each one of them has been generous with her time and comments.

Members of my Baltimore writing group – Nora Frankiel, Emily Mitchell, Jill Morrow, Sherry Morrow, Shawn Sapp-Nocher – have offered consistent support and intelligent critique.

The front cover of this volume is based on the magnificent stained-glass window created by Willet Studios (now Willet Hauser Architectural Glass, Inc.) of Philadelphia, PA, for the First Presbyterian Church in Belmont, NC. Special thanks to Pastor Samuel P. Warner of the church and James A. Hauser, Vice President of Willet Hauser, for permission to use this wonderful creation.

And finally, I want to thank my publishers: Alexandria Szeman, for her powerful literary vision, creativity, support and love in bringing this, my first novel, to the public through RockWay Press; and Gray Matter Imprints, which is issuing this second edition of *The Binding* after last year publishing The *Rabbi's Husband* and soon a new edition of *Full Speed. Full Stop.*

PART ONE

. . Abraham built an altar there;
he laid out the wood; he bound his son Isaac;
he laid him on the altar, on top of the wood.
And Abraham picked up the knife to slay his son.

Genesis 22:9-10

CHAPTER ONE

Dave Razkowski fell from the rock face he'd been climbing and the world slowed down. He had enough time to think clearly, even to plan. He had time to call her name, "Robin." There was even a moment to repeat their young daughter's name, "Sunny."

Falling, Dave consciously jettisoned his backpack. He got rid of his climbing axe too, trying to throw it so that he wouldn't land on one of the sharp points. With the reflexes of a natural athlete he maneuvered his body in space so that he wouldn't break his neck on impact. Near the bottom of the fall his sense of speed increased. The rock face hurtled past him. Even then he experienced something of a floating sensation, as though the cool early-morning air heating on the rocks and beginning to rise in thermals supported him a little.

But nothing cushioned Dave's landing. It was hard and direct, in the narrow, flat area at the base of his climbing site.

Weeks later, when he could finally admit that he remembered the details of his fall, the first thing he told Robin was that he had called out for her.

CHAPTER TWO

Wolff Blumen began each leg of his flight in the identical manner. He made sure his skullcap sat squarely on top of his head. He said a short, almost wordless prayer. Then he pulled at each long curly earlock in turn to straighten it, so that he could tuck it firmly behind his ear. After that he settled his earphones. Finally he clamped the whole construction in place — his curly black hair, the skullcap, the earlocks and the earphones — by setting his black fedora extra-firmly, straight on his head.

Even after a decade it was difficult for him to believe that he had a job that included piloting an airplane. Being the *Rav*'s choice to learn to fly made up for so many of the things he'd sacrificed.

People who were new to the area were always surprised to see an identifiable Orthodox Jew flying the Cherokee Six. The regulars no longer gave it a thought.

He had started out early in the morning leaving Sioux Falls where he lived for Kearney, Nebraska, the center for his deliveries from Grand Island to North Platte.

It was barely noon. Today everything had gone smoothly. He'd been in and out of the Kearney airstrip in less than half an hour. His next destination was Rapid City, in the far west of the state.

So today he had time; time to bomb the railroad tracks that took the trains to the Nazi death-camp, Auschwitz. It's full name Auschwitz-Birkenau: *Auschwitz*, the concentration-work camp near the Polish village Oswiecim, the part of the camp where inmates were starved worked or beaten to death; and Birkenau, *"Grove of Birch Trees,"* sometimes called *Auschwitz II*, the area of the camp where the gas chambers and crematoria were, the section of the camp that had only one purpose – genocide, racial extermination.

Maybe this time in his bombing raid, Wolff would save his parents. Then his pain would never have been born. He would never have been born.

Even if the Allies wouldn't do it, he would. He would destroy the train tracks to the concentration camps. Millions would live.

He brought his Cherokee down as if setting up for a strafing run when a cold flash of light penetrated like a bullet through his windshield, square into his eyes, momentarily blinding him. In urban areas skylights and other rooftop structures often flashed, but he always ignored them. In this vicinity a flash was totally unexpected. His first thought was that it must be deliberate. But, how could that be? There was no one down there.

Curious, he returned to his original heading; he saw it again, a brief but bright gleam coming from the brown rocks in a small, canyon-like structure. The source of the sun-bright signal was a tool, an instrument of some kind, wedged into the rocks. That was what had reflected the sun. At the same moment, he realized what had caused the flash: a man lying on the ground a few feet away.

Amazed, his imaginary bombing run now forgotten, Wolff angled the plane, trying to look even more sharply down. The rim of his fedora bumped against the small side window and was knocked askew, dislodging his earphones.

This was no time for incompetence! He grabbed for his hat but dislodged his skullcap. At the same time the earlock behind his left ear loosened and tangled in his long, square beard.

He calmed himself as he kept his airplane circling. Moving very deliberately, he placed his black fedora on the passenger seat beside him, where it would be out of the way, meanwhile pushing his skullcap roughly back in place, although he thought that God, *Hashem*, the Holy Name Above, would understand a bare head at such a moment. He recalled exactly what he needed to do from his long-ago flight training. He punched the correct frequency, 122.4, and reported to Huron Flight Radio, the closest facility.

They acknowledged his signal immediately. Wolff responded. "This is N2763 Poppa. I've got a climber down. I'm at 24 DME, unable to land. He's in a small canyon, miles from any road that I can see. He's not moving at all. How fast can you get Air Rescue here, Huron? If there's any chance for him, I think it has to be very fast. I say again. This is N2763 Poppa with a sighting of a downed climber."

✡

Dave's mind cleared again. For the moment he knew he was lying on the narrow gritty ledge at the base of the rock face that had been his objective for Thursday. He was in one of the least-accessible areas of Badlands National Park, the Palmer Creek Unit. It was true wilderness, far from the polite tourist areas with ever-present Park Rangers, paved highways, and Mount Rushmore.

While he could think straight, he reviewed his situation: no one knew his location, and the four-wheel-drive Jeep Wrangler that served him as base camp was at least two miles away. He'd had to hike in to reach this spot.

How ironic to be lying in the exact place where he'd stood to plan the day's climb, as though he hadn't started out yet.

It must be hours since he fell, even though it felt like only seconds. He'd started his climb shortly after dawn, when the sun was still hidden behind the surrounding rocks' eastern aspect. Now a summer-hot sun blazed high in the sky, full in his eyes. He could feel sunburn in the taut skin on his face, in the prickle of his eyelids. He knew he was badly hurt; he couldn't even raise a hand to shield his eyes.

That intense effort, the pain of trying to move, tumbled him into a dream-like state. He'd felt like this before, although he wasn't sure when. Now he was uncertain of what was happening around him, or exactly where he'd landed. In some ways the dream-state was better. He didn't worry, and there was less pain. He called out for his family again; this time as if they were near-by and might actually hear him.

"Robin.

"Sunny."

Empty South Dakota Badlands, a Mars landscape of jumbled rocks, stretched away in every direction. He was on the Pine Ridge Indian Reservation located partially within the Park. But unless someone had a purpose like Dave's own in mind, there was no reason to travel this way. The populated areas were miles away: Rapid City in the West, Sioux Falls and Minneapolis to the north and east. But, as the sun blasted down from its ever-higher position in the sky, Dave could no longer have pointed out which way was east and which way west.

Lying on the rocky outcrop, he struggled to call himself back to reality. It occurred to him that if Robin had to bury him, she would have a minister. She wouldn't know to call a rabbi. She didn't know he was Jewish. She wouldn't know how to get in touch with his family, unless she went through his private papers first thing. She wouldn't do that. Robin wouldn't even go into his office until she absolutely had to. He'd always kept his office and all its secrets as private as possible.

But, at that moment he had other things to worry about. He couldn't feel specific parts of his body, no matter how he willed it. There were just diffuse areas of pain. Neither hand would move, nor could he think of how to make his legs respond.

Being paralyzed or dying was not acceptable. There had to be something he could do, some action he could take.

He had landed slightly on his side, so he thought that perhaps his right arm didn't work because it was wedged beneath him. But his left arm was free. It ought to move. He concentrated on that. Except for fresh pain, there was no response.

Nearby, just off to his right, a green sliver of color and further away, the cold, white flash of sunlight on metal, both alien in his present all-stone world, told him where his backpack and climbing axe had landed. He felt a certain triumph; they were on the ledge with him. He had judged accurately. The ledge was only about ten or twelve feet wide, so he might easily have sent his equipment over the edge, forty feet down to the base-rock surface.

At least he was out in the open. He wouldn't die in a dark, cramped, boxcar-like place, where all the rest of them had died. His father always described the camps and the approach to the camps as if they were the only places a Jew could die. It would not happen to him. They would never get him. He'd made sure of that, with these trips, with everything he'd built in the house as protection. Ever since he was a kid he'd thought about dying a lot, from the first moments his father had told him about all the ways people died in the concentration camps.

Was he only imagining this outdoor place, this world of rock and stone? Maybe he really was in a boxcar on his way...

His father had survived two camps, Buchenwald and Mathhausen. Beyond survival, his father had been lucky in one other way. The concentration camps had been his father's test. One overwhelming test was enough to last a lifetime. Was this his test?

How could he find out, when just trying to move left him cold and perspiring at the same time? At least he didn't imagine that his left arm actually did move a little. He was still alive. He could hear and see too.

How had he managed to save his backpack, to get it on to this boxcar? These stone walls didn't fool him.

He knew where he was heading. But there was the airplane. Maybe it would save him. No. No airplane had ever bombed the train tracks, so why would this one? Nothing would stop this boxcar.

He couldn't acknowledge the airplane anyway. It had to be kept secret. His father had taught him that in the camps secrets were life itself: where you kept your food, who was a friend. All the important things were secret. Just like the secrets in his house that would save Robin and Sunny and the rest of his family. Except, maybe he should have told…

He couldn't even think of telling his secrets. At that thought the plane flew on and Dave was alone on his nightmare journey.

CHAPTER THREE

By Thursday all Robin wanted was to stay in bed and avoid people.

But she had to get Sunny to school, and she had to teach her nine-thirty aerobics class. Her job at the North Woods Sports Club was too good to risk just because she was worried.

She'd worried ever since Dave left the previous Saturday morning. Taking the past as a measure, she would worry until Dave got home. She always worried during the first week of September, and always about the same thing.

There was no point staying in bed with a pillow over her head. That wouldn't bring Dave home. It wouldn't even get him to a telephone.

In the staff dressing room at North Woods she tried to concentrate on getting her new shoes just right, with the laces perfectly even. Everyone at work thought she was shy, so they probably wouldn't notice if she seemed even quieter than usual.

Noelle, one of the other instructors, stopped kidding with her buddy Arlene long enough to size up Robin's new exercise outfit.

"Hey! Hot Stuff. Honestly Robin, gray and pink? Where do you find these things? Don't you think people expect something livelier from their aerobics instructor?"

Robin hated the kind of thing Noelle was wearing, although she would never say that. Robin thought most of her colleagues were ten years behinds, stuck in the 80's when it came to fashion. Today Noelle was wearing an abstract-patterned leotard in hot pink, purple and turquoise cut thong style, over hot pink tights.

In Fargo the boss had insisted that all the girls wear brightly colored cropped tops and thongs. He'd had a lot to say about fit too. She had never argued. At five foot five and a hundred and ten pounds, she knew she could wear the extreme styles, but her preference was for what a ballet dancer might wear, like her new gray leotard.

She smiled at Noelle as she pulled a North Woods T-shirt over her outfit. She wasn't going to start a debate. Her friendships at work might seem casual, but they were too important to risk. She and Dave rarely had people over to the house. Dave preferred to spend his time with her or with Sunny, or to work upstairs in his office, experimenting with his computer. He was willing to take her out though, as long as it was just the two of them. He'd happily take her to any movie she wanted to see, a rock concert, or out for dinner. She knew it was his way of making up for their isolation.

Noelle smiled back at Robin. "Well, you've got a guy. I suppose less sexy is less competition for the rest of us."

Her boss in Fargo thought that way too; that everything at a sports club had to do with sex, from the exercise routines to the menu in the health bar. After she'd been with Dave awhile she'd realized that the boss actually knew nothing about sex, about how it could be between a man and a woman.

On an ordinary day little things like the conversations in the dressing room, along with the perfect fit and feel of her new shoes, were enough to make Robin feel satisfied. She remembered when she couldn't afford decent exercise clothes or shoes.

Now she got new shoes whenever she needed them. Dave said they were a business expense. He insisted she buy the best. She'd bought her new shoes while shopping for clothes and school supplies with Sunny. They'd even found Sunny a pair of sneakers that looked just like hers, with the same pink and gray trim.

Noelle turned back to her conversation with Arlene, leaving Robin feeling bereft. But she couldn't think of a thing to say that would keep Noelle, Arlene, or anyone else talking to her.

It was the first week of school for Sunny, and Dave hadn't even been willing to stay in the city to be a part of that milestone. Education was so important to Dave that Robin had half expected that this year she'd succeed in getting him to cancel or delay his annual trip. It hadn't worked. Not only that, the resulting explosion from Dave when she'd asked him to stay home, had pretty much told her that she would never be able to get him to cancel. She would just have to live with it. If Dave's devotion to Sunny was insufficient, then nothing would work.

Dave had been taking his trip during Labor Day week each of the seven years she'd known him, and before that too. Nothing bad had ever happened. Somehow, though, that knowledge failed to calm her. There were too many mysteries about the trip. He always went alone. For some reason, canceling or changing the date was totally non-negotiable. She used to wonder what would have happened if her due date for Sunny had been in early September rather than later in the month.

As she left the staff locker room, Robin made a silent promise. Next year she wouldn't say a single word when Dave left. She wouldn't even let on that she worried.

Dave revived again to wind in his face and to an angel hovering overhead. His angel—the angel his father said watched over every person—had come.

Dave couldn't see his angel's features because the sun was straight up behind him. But he could see the angel's wings, a rotating nimbus. Here he was dying and he'd never thought to leave a message for Robin. And now he knew something that no one else knew: angels flew like helicopters, not like birds. Unfortunately, he had no way to tell anyone.

The angel stood over him. He'd brought rescue equipment along. Dave's angel had an extra-light plastic and aluminum stretcher. That had to be some kind of a trick, because Dave never needed rescuing. He rescued other people, not vice-versa. Sometimes Robin said he'd rescued her. She meant something else when she said that, like gratitude.

Dave wasn't grateful for this rescue. In fact, he started to protest that he didn't need help, but no words came. It was just like when he tried to talk to Robin, when he tried to get the right words out. The words never came.

"Robin."

He couldn't even think of the other words he had to say; just that they were important.

"Robin?"

But she wasn't anywhere nearby. Even in his present state Dave knew he was the one who'd made sure that she never came climbing with him, and that she didn't know anything about this trip. His habit of secrecy ran so deep that he'd forgotten she might actually need to know some things. Now it was too late.

The angel dropped to his knees alongside Dave. "Hey, don't! Don't do that. Don't try to move until we know what's broken. Lie still. Just lie still."

Dave only wanted to tell the angel that he couldn't move, but even those words didn't come. Then he thought that even though this was a very young angel, only about twenty, he should know if someone was paralyzed.

The rescue angel got very busy. It seemed that he tried to understand what Dave was saying, but at the same time he opened his kit and began to take Dave's vital signs. He said, "What did you say? Are you checking up on how well we do things? Are you in pain?"

Then hard pain thundered over Dave and he remembered that he had felt that before, more than once, in the short time he'd been there. Or maybe he'd been lying on these rocks much longer than he realized, for such hot pain to come back more than once.

Pain was secret. Pain was the biggest secret of all. You could die if you admitted to pain. He was positive that in the camps his father had never admitted to pain.

All of his life he'd been watching his father light those hundreds of *yarzheit* candles to memorialize the dead.

That was pain. But his father never said a word. Every year his father brought death right into their house, remembering his family and his comrades who'd died in the camps. He never flinched. He looked pinched and worn all that memorial week, this week, the first week in September. But he never showed fear. Dave had learned to hide that small fear of his too—the fear he felt for his father, and for himself. So now he would say something clever to throw his angel off the trail. But whatever he tried to say slurred first in his mind, and then in his mouth.

"Hey, I said don't try to move by yourself. I'll do it!" His angel really meant what he said. Dave had to follow orders, even though he would die anyway. In his father's stories almost everyone died.

The thought flashed: *I don't ever have to do this again.*

That was when Dave slipped back from consciousness into some other place, a place more fearsome to him than falling from a mountain, or even dying.

In that place all his worst dreams—his strenuously-denied dreams—resided. In his dreams they would come for him and kill him. Over and over again they killed him, along with his father and his mother, because they were all Jews, and because they were together. Men in uniforms would kill his whole family; it was only a question of where and when.

But they wouldn't know about Sunny. He'd thought of everything. Robin was Sunny's mother. Robin wasn't Jewish, so Sunny wasn't, either. It wasn't a guarantee, but it might save her. Robin might be able to protect Sunny. The house itself was the final ring of protection for all of them. But he hadn't told Robin what she needed to know. She didn't know about the men in uniforms.

He looked up. His angel wore a uniform too. So when the angel put a firm, controlling hand on him and said, "Don't try to move," something deep inside compelled Dave to struggle against that order.

His struggles made his angel turn his face up to the sky to pray.

Dave thought: I could help him. I know the right prayer for dying; and the prayer for those who are dead.

But the angel didn't pay any attention to his prayers. It was exactly what his father said: prayers are only for the dead, because they expect them to be recited.

Dave's angel wasn't praying. He was talking to a second angel coming down the line from heaven. Dave tried to think clearly, to grapple with everything whirling around him.

When he tried to consider what two angels instead of one might mean, his mind ricocheted outside his control. His father had told him about some miraculous rescues in the camps. Angels, he'd said, there was no other possible explanation. He'd never actually seen an angel in the camps, only known that they were there. He certainly didn't know about angels' wings.

The lead rescue worker reported to his dispatcher.

"He's delirious, and dehydrated. But his vitals are still pretty good. He's a tough one. At minimum there are several fractured vertebrae, clavicle, pelvis and a shattered right leg. We'll take him straight to Sioux Falls. They have the ortho he's going to need. Line up Haines for the surgery."

Then he turned to his assistant. "Hold him, although he doesn't much like that. Can you tell what he's trying to say? A lot of it isn't English. The rest is names mostly, Robin, and something else."

Dave opened his eyes again briefly: *more than one angel for me.*

CHAPTER FOUR

olff made a flawless landing at the small private airport just south of Sioux Falls, barely raising the dust. He taxied over to the packed-earth area where he kept his plane, in front of one of the small, corrugated metal storage sheds. He'd just received word that the man he'd helped rescue was being brought to the Sioux Falls Hospital. Wolff was on duty there later, so he'd have plenty of time to visit.

He glanced at his watch. Only three o'clock. He had time to deliver the rent check for the plane and even a few moments to savor the day.

Any day when he had saved a life had to be like this: the sky blue, the wind-sock billowing lazily in a soft breeze from the west, the white paint and the red stripes on his airplane shining, crisp and clean. He felt just like when he'd been on stage and had hit his mark every time.

The traditional blessing, *Baruch HaShem*, the Holy One, blessed be His Name, bubbled to his lips, praise for helping him see the downed climber. Today he understood what his teachers of *Torah* and *Talmud* meant when they insisted that people look for miracles in the wrong places. Most miracles are just the everyday surprises in a good life.

Wolff Blumen considered his whole life a miracle. As for surprises, he enjoyed the surprise he presented to the world. He looked antique, but when people got to know him they realized that an Orthodox Jew could be very contemporary. And, although his life wasn't as dramatic as when he'd been a performer, the impact he made now lasted much longer. Now he had a great part for life, instead of just for an evening.

He even liked South Dakota. If he hadn't lived there, many people would never even have met a Jew. So, while he knew that the isolation from extended family and from a larger Jewish community was hard on his wife and his children, he was content. He was sure that one day they would all be rewarded for their time in South Dakota, and would be able to return to their community in New York.

It would have to be before his oldest son turned thirteen. Otherwise he and Faiga would need to send Shalom away to a *Yeshiva* for schooling. Wolff would never survive such a separation.

But, for the time being, there were compensations in South Dakota. He was positive that when anti-Semites sounded off with their crackpot theories about world conspiracies and Christ-killers, the men he worked with would defend him. Therefore they would be defending all Jews.

He could imagine what it would be like. Jerry Rales, Tom Whitely, or Chief, the man who owned the airstrip, would say, "Na, you don't know what you're talking about. This Jewish guy I know, Rabbi Blumen, he's a great guy."

Wolff wasn't actually a Rabbi, but no one in Sioux Falls seemed to understand that. To them, any man who looked like him must be a Rabbi. Long ago Wolff had given up explaining that his role in the Jewish community was important, but more humble than that of a Rabbi.

Wolff was a *shoichet*, a ritual slaughterer of animals for kosher meat. He and his family lived in Sioux Falls, one of very few Orthodox families in the tiny Jewish community. They were there because the huge meat-packing plant in Sioux Falls employed ritual slaughterers, who were always from among the Orthodox.

Kosher meat was shipped all over the country from South Dakota, to all cities with large Jewish populations. But before Wolff's arrival kosher meat didn't reach the small communities right in the area, because the amounts needed weren't sufficient for the plant to bother.

Making kosher meat and other supplies available in the area had been the *Rav*'s idea. He was the leader of Wolff's sect of Orthodox Judaism.

The *Rav* had wanted someone to deliver supplies. Wolff's father-in-law, who worked for the *Rav*, wanted to teach Faiga and Wolff a lesson. Sending them to some isolated post was the perfect way to do that. So Wolff had been assigned to the job.

Back in New York, the *Rav* had been the one who arranged for Wolff to train as a *shoichet* when he'd chosen to leave his old life as a performer. Also, he'd arranged for the necessary flying lessons in Sioux Falls. Neither Wolff nor Faiga could have imagined they would still be living in Sioux Falls ten years later.

The *Rav* considered Wolff perfect for the job, newly returned to Judaism, and idealistic about what could be accomplished. And the wishes of Rabbi Goldfein, Wolff's father's-in-law, were respected. Faiga had dared to marry Wolff even though her parents disapproved. She'd argued for her marriage with her father, and she'd won the argument. So be it, Rabbi Goldfein said. They were married. But Faiga had to know that girls did not make inappropriate marriage choices without cost. Wolff had to understand that marrying into a family like the Goldfeins didn't provide instant acceptance for someone so ignorant, someone's whose commitment to Orthodox Judaism was as yet unproven.

Wolff had only been observant a brief period of time when they were married. He'd not yet had time to become a serious student, let alone a learned man. He'd spent his childhood on the stage, not studying *Torah* and *Talmud*. When he embraced the Orthodox life, he'd had to start with the Hebrew alphabet, *aleph-bet,* what is normally taught to children. Reb Goldfein made sure that Wolff realized that only great effort and years of patient study, would earn a place of equality and respect.

So Wolff studied with Faiga, and on his own. He taught his children what he learned. He continued to work in the packing plant and to make his deliveries. Over the years he had expanded the number of small towns he visited. He'd even increased the demand for kosher products. Now he flew a regular schedule to International Falls, Detroit Lakes, Bemidji and Duluth in Minnesota. Closer to home he took increasing amounts of goods to Rapid City and to Kearney.

Wolff knew that a flying *shoichet* was even more unusual than a flying rabbi. Of course no one in the

Midwest cared whether he was a rabbi or not. In New York he was too ignorant to even study for the title of Rabbi. In his present community that status was freely granted.

Wolff gave the small plane a final pat when he'd finished pulling on the canvas cover that protected it. He parked in a slightly out-of-the-way corner of the small airstrip, part of a flying club centered on an old World War II training field. There were only two active runways left, crossing each other. In most places the grass grew so thick it had destroyed all the seventy-year-old cement. A hundred and fifty years of settlement had hardly made a difference in large parts of the prairies.

Almost all the temporary buildings that had housed the Air Force were gone—the shelters, the barracks, the Quonset huts. With a single exception, even the buildings meant to be permanent had been dismantled, the work of snow and howling winds rather than of any orderly plan.

Surprisingly, Wolff had found flight training easy, soul-satisfying, like learning *Torah*, the Five Books of Moses. He'd qualified as a pilot at the same time he'd begun the serious study of *Torah*, so the two were linked in his mind, a *Torah* for the world, a *Torah* for flight. He'd proved be an excellent student.

He hadn't known that he could be good at anything except performing. While he was growing up his parents' major obsession in life had been the safety of their little family, the three of them. When the Nazi's came back— his parents were certain they would be back—Wolff's career as William Flowers, a performer, was their only possibility of survival. The constant travel, being able to hide, the new name they'd all adopted, might save them. The travel of Wolff's early years–and his parents' ideas about survival–had made everything about his childhood haphazard and miserable.

Now it was wonderful to be Wolff Blumen, a husband and father, a good pilot and a student of *Torah*. The *Torah* had come alive for him from the first moment. He loved that with *Torah* as with a play, memory was not enough. To really understand you had to be able to interpret.

Finally, satisfied with how he was leaving his plane, Wolff headed for the only original Air Force building left standing. It housed Bess' Coffee Shop and the flight club office.

The moment he walked into the coffee shop it was clear that everyone had heard about the rescue. People at the small airport were always friendly; but today they looked up with admiration. One of the men drinking coffee clapped him on the shoulder as he walked past the booths near the door.

"Good job, Rabbi!"

"Atta boy."

"That's one damn lucky guy, you spotting him like that. That had to be a one-in-a-million chance."

Bess, Chief's wife, stood in the serving area of the U-shaped counter. With her brass-gold hair and pink spots of rouge on her cheeks, Bess suited the coffee shop's late 1940's décor perfectly.

The little restaurant had yellow or red marbleized Formica on almost every surface; all of it edged with heavily ribbed chrome. The trim had been there so long there was grime in every ridge and seam. Somehow it wasn't offensive. It seemed to belong there, like black oil under a mechanic's fingernails.

Bess liked to serve up the very latest news with every meal. News was dessert to people at the strip, as much as a piece of her homemade pie. Anyone who wanted to do business with Chief had to report to Bess first, as they walked through the coffee shop on the way to the office.

"Nice!" Bess said, offering an enthusiastic thumbs-up.

"Good work, Rabbi. Let me stand you to a coffee," one of the pilots said.

Wolff appreciated that, especially from a veteran flyer.

"The usual?" Bess asked. Wolff nodded, and thanked her when she brought him a can of Coke and a paper cup.

"Wouldn't you rather have coffee?" said Wolff's admirer. "I'll stand you to a piece of pie, too. What the hell, you don't help save a guy's life every day."

Bess was self-important with knowledge. "He can't. He's kosher. He can't touch a thing that's on these dishes, nothing cooked or baked; can't eat in a single restaurant in town. All he can have is a soft drink from the can, or in a paper cup. Right, Rabbi?"

She seemed proud that Wolff had such high standards that he couldn't eat her food.

"Right," Wolff said. "Believe me; I really appreciate this Coke right now."

"Well, you saved that climber, no doubt. No one knew he was out there. Must be some stupid kid not to leave word or arrange for a pick up. And you actually spot him just lying there at the base of a rock face. I wonder how far he'd fallen. That's a bad area. I know it. He could have been forty, fifty feet up, even more. Amazing, he wasn't killed right off. You were led there, that's for sure."

"Absolutely, I agree," Wolff said, chug-a-lugging the last of his soft drink.

"Thanks for the Coke and the good thoughts."

He actually got a small round of applause as he walked back through to Chief's office. He'd never thought he'd hear that directed toward him again.

CHAPTER FIVE

Wolff left Chief's office for his van, suddenly utterly weary, although his day was far from done. Wolff served as a hospital chaplain in addition to being a *shoichet*. He needed several jobs to earn enough money for his family. The meatpacking plant paid him for the ritual slaughter of animals, *sh'cheitah,* and there was also some money every month from the *Rav*, payment for making the deliveries. But he and Faiga never had quite enough.

When they'd married he'd said, "I'll be like Jacob, working seven years, even twice seven years, for the girl. But I get the girl while I'm doing it, so it's better for me than it was for him." He still felt that way, basically, although sometimes the lack of money was frustrating. Usually he just told himself it was part of all that he needed to learn.

Being a chaplain was a good extra job. It taught him a lot about real people and their troubles.

The *Rav* believed that a chaplain did not have to be a rabbi, and he'd managed to convince the State of South Dakota on that point. No one in the area was any better qualified than Wolff. The job combined well with his other responsibilities. When he was in distant parts of the state making deliveries, he could also visit the Jews who were in the prisons, in the state mental hospital and in out-of-the-way nursing homes.

As chaplain, he held a staff position at the Sioux Falls General Hospital. He was not just the chaplain for Jewish patients, but a general chaplain as well. He was on call every Sunday, plus a few nights or evenings a week. This was exactly when Wolff was most readily available, and when the Christian clergy was the busiest.

He had a shift to work on Friday, an exhausting thought at that moment. He didn't even have the energy for his usual jaunty swing up into the cab of his van. This time it was a laborious climb. Once inside he just sat there. He didn't even put the key in the ignition. His original sense of jubilation was fading. He had to collect his thoughts, to make sense of his feelings.

He knew why he felt so tired, so cold. Every time he made one of his ersatz bombing runs he was replaying his family's history. Despite the brief excitement of the fantasy, in the end he was always left feeling useless. There had been no rescue then. There was nothing he could do to change history. Even today, the adrenaline rush, the joy of the real-life rescue, couldn't totally counteract the despair he still felt when he considered his parents' lives.

Sometimes, while flying, he would weave long, imaginary scenes, dramas of what his parents' lives would have been if they'd had an airplane and a pilot like him in Poland. If they'd had a small airplane they could have flown away, escaped, instead of ending up in one of Hitler's accursed boxcars on the way to Auschwitz. But who in wartime Poland had access to a private airplane?

As those thoughts flooded through him he knew what he had to do. Right there, sitting in his van, he closed his eyes to focus on the spiritual exercises the *Rav* had given him. He visualized the words of *Torah* that were his mantra, as though they were printed out before him in flaming letters. He could warm himself there. The repetition of those words thousands of times in the last decade had allowed him to ease away from the dark side of his soul. Those words were his map. It had taken years, but he had built a road away from his deepest despair.

The *Rav* had said he should concede that he'd had a difficult childhood as William Flowers. But he also had to recognize the compensations for his childhood. Now he had a good marriage, children, and a manner of living that made order of the chaos his childhood had left behind. Wolff had found a life commanded by God. That made him one of the lucky ones, blessed.

When he felt better, warm again, he started the van and pulled out of the parking lot. Now he was enough at peace to drive in his usual manner—as though, if he went fast enough, the van would fly up like his beloved plane. The van hurtled over the rough road. It had been one of the old bare-earth landing strips that happened to lead to the highway. Nothing had been done to improve it, so a black-brown cloud of prairie dust billowed around the van, filling the sky behind him.

Would his fantasy always plague him? Would he always dream of saving his parents and their first families from the camps? He must finally, firmly, believe that he could never save the lives of those half brothers and sisters of his who had died in the camps years before his birth.

His vehicle rattled over the uneven ruts in the road. The shocks were old. He felt every irregular bump.

"Save a life and it is as if you save the whole world." He mused out loud over that quote as though that was his mantra, or as though he was engaged in the study of it.

Suddenly he slammed on his brakes. The van shuddered and stopped. The vibrations stilled. No airplanes flew overhead at that moment. All was quiet.

He had just saved a life!

Pickuach h'nefesh. Saving a life was a gift from *Hashem*; His most extraordinary gift. It was the one *mitzvah* that surpassed all others and all circumstances. It had just been granted to him!

Another realization tumbled in quickly behind the first. Wolff experienced a special clarity, an understanding of what the rescue really meant. His teachers had told him that sometimes such moments came, but only if one had studied long enough and hard enough. Instead of a confusion of questions in his mind he heard the rhythms of the *yeshiva* in his head, setting out what had just happened. The discussion was actually audible, as though it was on the radio, in the singsong 'if-then' rhetoric of the *yeshiva*'s hall of study.

If this is a rational world, then I cannot possibly save anything or anybody who is in the past.

But, if I've saved the life of this climber, then that is to say I have saved this world.

And, if this is the world of my children, then I have saved their world.

His own safety, the safety of any children he might have, had been the reasons Wolff became an Orthodox Jew in his thirties. He'd had to do something to feel secure, to heal the wounds of his childhood.

He was certain that his need for such a life had brought Rabbi Goldfein, Faiga's father, to him. Knowing Rabbi Goldfein had brought him Faiga. Faiga had really saved his life. Her love and her confidence in him had accomplished it. Magically, she'd been willing to marry him, even though her parents disapproved. Now he'd always have her steadfast presence. She hadn't saved his life once, the way Rabbi Goldfein had when he'd recognized his suicidal state of mind. Faiga saved him every day of their life together.

Wolff started up the van again. Driving very slowly now, meditatively, he turned onto the highway. An astounding, miraculous thing had just happened, and he might have missed it; just as he might have missed the climber.

Except, thanks to God he had not.

Surprisingly he felt no immediate need to share his thoughts with Faiga. He didn't even want to tell any of his teachers at that moment. He wouldn't have told the *Rav* himself, even if he had been sitting right beside him in the van. He needed to understand fully before he shared this with anyone. He had to think it all through on his own.

The feeling of joy did not fade away as he drove to his home. This was real. All he wanted to do was praise God. He thought of his children. Telling his children about saving a life would be the best lesson ever.

He'd only learned fear as a child. He'd never tell his children that the Nazis would be back. He would never say that if all else failed, if he couldn't protect them, then he would kill them before committing suicide himself. His parents had said that to him all the time. That plan had been the greatest gift they could imagine.

His children would have a real gift, utterly different from his inheritance. His children would be strong through joy in their belief in *Hashem*, through knowledge of their Judaism. In his mind he began to rehearse his story, the joy of seeing the man, knowing that he had saved him.

He would not tell them about his bombing raids, pretending to blow up the train tracks to the camp. That was a part of his bitter inheritance, to be endured, not passed along.

But something more had just happened to him, although he didn't quite understand it. Sharing it would have to wait until he understood it himself.

It was odd to have something that he didn't immediately tell his wife. Wolff and Faiga were unusual among Orthodox couples. They had not been introduced to each other in the traditional way: by friends, by a family member, or by a matchmaker. They had accidentally come to know each other when her father had brought Wolff home for what should have been a brief, emergency visit. But Wolff's charm had affected even Reb Goldfein and there had been that first invitation to stay for dinner.

Rabbi Goldfein often brought Jews in distress to his office, but they rarely met anyone in the family. No one would ever have predicted that Faiga, a respected Rabbi's daughter, would marry a Jew newly returned to religious life, a Jew as yet untested by years of practice. The opposition to their marriage had made a strong bond between them. It had never occurred to him that a woman would fight for him, but Faiga had done just that.

Their bond was such that eight months before, after the birth of their twins, Faiga had even been able to say that they had to do something to make a separate room for the babies. She was afraid that if they had two children sharing the master bedroom she would come to hate them. She'd been somewhat tearful, but firm. "It was okay with the others, but two babies in the room, it's too much. I'll never get any sleep. And we'll never get to…"

She was still shy about talking about sex, even though she wasn't at all shy about participating. Sex was a *mitzvah* for a married couple. They were supposed to enjoy the physical act of love.

Like other Orthodox women Faiga followed strict laws of modesty. She'd covered her own hair completely after marriage, with fashionable wigs. All her adult life she had dressed in skirts longer than knee length, with sleeves below her elbows, and necklines that were cut higher than the hollows of her collarbones. Like other women in her community a certain shyness, especially around discussions of physical intimacy, seemed to have developed from that modesty.

"Mrs. Blumen," Wolff had said at her oblique reference to making love, "Are you saying you don't want your children around because it will mess up our love-making?" He'd raised one eyebrow, just one, as he said that, and waggled it at her. It was a broad stage leer that always made her laugh. She'd flushed.

Then her normal forceful personality reasserted itself. "Yes I am."

"Well, we can't let that happen," Wolff said. "How much space do you think we can give up?" Their bedroom, which had already lost the space it had taken to create the second bathroom in the house, was subdivided again.

The resulting room was cramped and unattractive, but at least it was private.

Wolff knew that no woman but his Faiga would ever have admitted to the possibility of such a feeling about her children.

The two of them always tried to steal a few quiet minutes to talk together before they slept, often holding one conversation over several days. Their unconventional courtship, carried on during visits Wolff managed to arrange with Rabbi Goldfein, had taught them how to pick up and drop conversations without losing their central thought. Now, with the demands on their time from Wolff's work schedule and the needs of their children, that skill still served them well. They were in bed that Thursday night with the lights out, when Faiga referred back to the rescue.

"Baruch HaShem, what you said to the children was absolutely correct. If you had not known how to fly that man would certainly have died there. We must let the *Rav* know. And you must go and visit the man you saved. Will you be at the hospital tomorrow as usual?" She edged closer to him, sighed. "I like this room best when it's dark. Then you and I can talk, and at least I can imagine that it's beautiful."

He responded to her second comment, because he still didn't want to say a lot about the afternoon.

"Yes, it's pretty bad, isn't it? If we're going to be here much longer we will have to talk to the *Rav* about a larger place."

"Well, they let us go in that tiny two-bedroom apartment until I was seven months pregnant with Shayna. If she'd been a boy, we might still be there, just with another set of bunk beds. So I'm sure they think two bedrooms upstairs, our room, a tiny nursery and two whole bathrooms are enough for a family of eight."

"Well, we are managing. I'm sure we'll continue to manage. And how do we know it's a family of eight? More are certainly possible." He reached over and stroked her arm gently, then laid his hand flat on her belly. She giggled, patted his hand. Then she turned over, away from him. They were both tired, even though it was during the two weeks in the month when they could have made love, when they were not denied to each other under Holy Law.

He knew that Faiga had always been grateful to be able to talk plainly to him. She'd often said that that might have been why she hadn't married before she met him. She'd felt that with most men conversations would have been circuitous, subjects raised only at certain times or in a veiled fashion.

He'd insisted that she hadn't married before because God had ordained their marriage.

"I'm the one who told you what *bashert* meant," Faiga had said, teasing a little. But Wolff was always serious about what they meant to each other, about their marriage. They'd had to fight her family to marry. She'd had to argue with her father. "Even if you said it first, even if you had to teach me what it meant, it isn't any less true," Wolff reminded her.

Before he fell asleep Wolff felt he had to respond to Faiga's first comment too. He hoped he sounded casual, and that she was so sleepy that she wouldn't want to discuss it any further.

"I'm going to be at the hospital as usual tomorrow, so it will be no problem to see the man I spotted."

He got no response. Faiga was already asleep.

As he drifted to sleep, he thought that maybe visiting the man he'd helped save would give him a better idea of what his private miracle meant.

CHAPTER SIX

After four years as the TV anchor at KLON, it seemed to Al that he now spent as much time worrying about the budget as he spent on-air. He hated that part of his job. True he got lots of air time, but as senior staff he was expected to pick up the slack in all areas. He hadn't anticipated that the pressure to save money would get worse every year. There was nothing more he could learn in Sioux Falls. It was definitely time to move on.

When he'd been a radio announcer with no TV experience, he'd thought it would be easier to launch a national career from a small station. He'd figured that a good reporter would stand out more in a small place than in a bigger market. Maybe he'd been mistaken. Maybe he should have stayed in radio, where he'd been a lot more comfortable.

In radio, as long as he had a good, fully automated studio and a decent phone system, he could create programs on his own. He didn't have to worry about staff. He might never have become famous in radio—okay, he wasn't famous in TV either—but he wouldn't have been saddled with an accountant's job of keeping the budget in line, or a psychologist's job of keeping the news team happy.

"Captain" Dale, the station's happy-go-lucky, pilot/traffic/weatherman, sauntered up as Al read a story about a rescue in the western part of the State. Dale had seen the story too. Because of their first encounter, just being around Dale made Al nervous … as nervous as thinking about the worst days at home, when his mother had insisted they had to play "They're coming,' over and over again. But there was no compensating lesson of survival to be learned from Dale.

"Al, I'm going to take the chopper up and see what this rescue looks like from the air," Dale said, waving his wire copy at him. "Care to come along?"

"Come off it, Dale. You're not going anywhere and you know it." Al said. He held the identical page of copy. "What's the local angle on this one? Is your brother on the rescue team? Or maybe it's one of your girlfriends, this time?"

Dale grinned at him. What a dope, he actually thought that was funny.

"Well, a local guy spotted him. Isn't that enough?"

Al glanced at the copy again. Score one for Dale for a change. A chaplain from Sioux Falls General Hospital had reported the sighting.

"Good call," Al said. He tried to limit his compliments, so they would actually mean something. In this case at least, Dale was right. There might be an interesting local angle in a flying chaplain.

"I'll tell you what," Al said, as though Dale really had inspired an idea. "Find out when and where he's going to get back. If the timing's decent, go interview him at the airfield. Get lots of atmosphere, do it pilot-to-pilot. It'll be great. Ask him about the difficulties of spotting someone like that. He must have practically been on top of the victim. If you can schedule it for right after you do the traffic and the 'ON-High' weather this afternoon, you can even take him up and let him show you what it felt like. But just around here, not at the site."

"Why not let Jim and I actually go take a look? We'll get you great pictures."

Al said, acid, "That's Jim and me. And that 'look' and those pictures would cost us a couple of thousand dollars. The interview and an approximation are free. So is the grammar lesson. That's the best I can do."

Dale left without arguing. Al was careful not to let his relief show. He was grateful, too. If there had been a stronger local angle he would have had to fly with Dale, and he hated that more then anything.

His initial flight with Dale had been the first time he'd lost control in years. He knew that because it had never happened, not even on the day Kennedy was shot in 1963. That had been his family's most important practice of 'they're coming.' From that day on he'd been the best. He'd been ready every single time, in line with his jacket, boots, and backpack. His mother said he'd been the best, even though he was the youngest. That day he'd heard the raw reality in her voice, her absolute belief that this time they really were coming.

However, in Sioux Falls he'd missed the threat lurking in Dale's seemingly friendly offer.

No one had told him that the first flight for new staff at the station was an initiation rite. Al had wanted to look experienced and open to anything, so of course he'd agreed to the flight. After, he'd been forced to be a good sport and take the kidding.

"Come see what a prairie fire looks like from the sky," Dale had said. Once they were in the air, Dale did what Al later learned was his usual routine with newcomers, showing off with all the rolls, dives and maneuvers that were legal, and even a few that weren't. Al, like every other newcomer, had eventually thrown up. It had only happened once. Since then he didn't go anywhere with Dale unless he had Dramamine, and unless it was absolutely necessary. He never forgot anything that frightening.

As it developed, Al had to cover the story about the climber. By mid-afternoon the station had received the information that Air Rescue would bring the man to Sioux Falls for surgery. Apparently orthopedic care was more advanced at the local hospital than in Rapid City. That was a great local angle.

Since it might be necessary to interview a surgeon, he couldn't trust any of his reporters. It was September and all of them were brand new. Almost every September brought a batch of newly minted reporters to small town newspapers, TV and radio stations. They'd work in places like Sioux Falls for a year or two at most, serving their apprenticeships. Then they moved on. Owners liked the system because it kept salaries low.

A perennially young staff was the reason that stations and newspapers in small towns made sure they always had one experienced person like Al around. If anything important happened, he covered it.

He could send a kid or someone like Dale to talk to a pilot, but not to interview a surgeon. He didn't want it to look like he only had babies or a grease monkey on his staff.

Anyway, just as the airlift bearing the downed climber was arriving in Sioux Falls, Dale was buzzing the station helicopter over an accident site seventy-five miles to the east of the city. The accident involved a big rig and two passenger cars, one of them registered to a member of a local family. That kind of story required pictures.

"Sorry, Al," Dale shouted in his ear, over the noise of the helicopter's rotors above him, "but I got the info for you. The pilot already returned from his run. I missed him. The victim will be arriving at General any minute. They're taking him straight into surgery. I got us clearance at the landing pad."

Al rushed to the hospital with his cameraman. He didn't like last minute stuff; it was always a colossal nuisance. But anything was better than a helicopter sortie with Dale.

He didn't like outdoor assignments either, especially seven stories up. The black-surfaced roof surrounding the landing pad blasted the unseasonable September heat into his face. The prairie wind was even more insistent than at ground level.

He wouldn't be able to hear a thing under these circumstances. So much for the chance to do one of his special ON-The-Spot interviews.

They'd better get some good pictures. I've set the cameraman up perfectly. All he has to do is aim.

Al looked back. "Keep that thing tight on me," he hollered. Why did these yokels think people cared about landscape?

If the victim turned out to be even half-way decent looking, they needed a visual. And their timing was perfect. He ducked in under the still turning rotors, catching the rescue workers just as they lifted the victim's stretcher off the helicopter.

The guy was quite photogenic, tall and thin, with longish brown hair that moved in the gale created by the wind and the helicopter blades. They'd cut off most of his clothes and encased him in a transparent, inflated, plastic suit that kept him immobilized. He wore a huge cervical collar and his hands were restrained.

If he could get any sound under these circumstances, then marry it with what ought to be a decent shot, he might actually have a story. *God damn, it would be easier to just re-stage this whole thing.*

He glanced back at his cameraman again, but he was too far away to figure out exactly what the man was doing. *God damn, if that guy is missing any of this, I'll have his one good eye.*

"How bad?" Al hollered into the ear of the rescue worker who seemed to be in charge.

The kid didn't really want to take the time, but he cooperated.

"Plenty bad enough," he said over his shoulder. He even added mime, gesturing with one hand to his own head, back, hip and leg, to indicate the areas injured.

Al thought the patient would be totally unconscious, but he could see that his lips were moving. He also seemed to be trying to gesture with his left hand, the only part of his body not badly injured.

"Was he alone?" Al tried to question the second rescue worker, who stood beside the stationary stretcher, adjusting two plastic intravenous bags which dangled from a low-slung holder that kept them level just above the victim's head.

"No, he had a brass band with him."

"Just doing my job," Al said.

"Well, my job comes first."

Whoever ought to come first, they all had to wait a few minutes while a doctor examined the patient. Al gave up on any kind of an interview at all and settled for trying to catch what the victim was saying. He held his microphone next to the man's mouth and kept it there, even walking to the rooftop elevator with the paramedics when the receiving doctor finished his examination. He would have gone along with the medical team, all the way to surgery, but the doctor looked up and shook his head, a very definite no. Al was certain the rescue workers enjoyed watching the elevator door shut in his face.

Had it been worthwhile? Did he have even halfway useable audio? It would take a lot to clean up the tape, filter out the background wind and noise. But if this guy had mumbled a name of some babe, like the report had said, or, even if it were his kid's name, there might be a good angle.

He couldn't do anything fancy with the story of the climber for the early news. He rushed back to the station with just enough time for a quick wardrobe change and make up.

"A downed climber was found today, grievously injured, at the foot of a rock face he had apparently been climbing alone."

The late news report would be better, with pictures, but at least he'd had the opportunity to use a word like 'grievously' in a news report.

He made a call to the hospital after the news. They told him that the climber had survived surgery. That meant there would be at least one more story. Plus, he had a bonus. He'd be able to use some of the footage for a feature on how good orthopedic care was in Sioux Falls. That would headline an edition of the local early Sunday morning TV newsmagazine that he edited.

He preferred doing just about anything between news broadcasts to going home to his messy, depressing apartment. He skipped dinner to save calories then commandeered the audio console in the studio so he could work on his tape.

It took an hour, but Al managed to clean up the sound on the tape, to filter out enough of the helicopter noise and wind so that he could hear some of the words the climber had repeated over and over again.

Air Rescue had said that that climber had been quite coherent for most of the plane ride to Sioux Falls, but they couldn't give him anything for pain, since he had to go straight into surgery. The pain had caused him to slip into delirium. But even that hadn't dulled the persistence in his voice.

No wonder he'd survived. He had to be one stubborn bastard: stubborn enough to keep calling, stubborn enough to stay alive. He didn't seem to be the usual dumb jock, either. He'd called out in several languages.

First there was the name, just as the medic had reported from the site. "Robin," repeated again and again. The hospital or the police would find her. Then Al recognized some Russian on the tape, the kind of thing his own grandmother called nursery language, largely the same cautions his father had repeated over and over during his childhood: Be careful. Not so fast. You'll hurt yourself.

Funny what his family worried about, even though they thought the Nazi would be back, or that the Communists would come and bomb the United States one day.

Then on the tape Al heard an explosion of guttural sounds that had to be German; broken curses, orders and demands, as though from a camp, *"Sie dreckiger Hund. Sei sind ein Schew."* That had made the hair on Al's neck stand up. In his house any word of German had been forbidden.

The last moments on the tape brought the biggest surprise of all, pieces of the most important Hebrew prayer, the *Sh'ma*: "Hear, Oh Israel, the Lord your God, the Lord is One." The thing you were supposed to say when you thought you were dying.

The muscles of Al's face congealed with fear. This was just like one of those unguarded moments at home, in the bathroom, or while doing his homework, or even when he was sound asleep when 'they're coming,' sounded in his ear.

You had to be dead to have control of your face all the time. What if someone from the station had actually been in the studio just then? What if he'd started working on the tape earlier in the day when others were around? There were a couple of other Jews on staff. Even in South Dakota it had caught up with him. Seeing his reaction, they would have realized that he understood. Al had trouble keeping a poker face around this kind of stuff, which was why he avoided other Jews.

When he'd still worked at WBBM in Chicago, there had been one of those Jewish sidewalk missionaries and their '*mitzvah* van' always parked in the Loop.

"Are you Jewish?" the rabbis who worked in the van would ask men walking by. They were interested in re-claiming Jews to active observance.

At first Al always said "no" if they asked him. Usu-ally, it didn't even come up. Even before his surgery he hadn't looked particularly Jewish. It bothered him to lie about it though, as though he felt ashamed, instead of just being careful.

Just once, after a particularly disturbing conversation with his mother, he'd answered "yes." He told himself he ought to see if there might be a story in the van. Then the men had expected him to go inside the van and *'lay t'fillen,'* put on the phylacteries observant Jewish men wore during weekday morning prayers.

Al never wrote that story. Once inside with his jacket off, he'd felt as though the walls and ceil-ing were closing in. The terror of that childhood game—he still had trouble believing they'd called it a game—flashed through his mind. "They're coming. What will you do?"

Al always thought he should have answered back, at least once. He could have said, "What did you do? They got you. You didn't escape," to his father or grandmother.

In the van his tutor had started quickly, speaking fast as he placed the first phylactery on Al's upper arm. Then the second black, box-like phylactery was placed on his forehead.

It was when his teacher returned to his arm to wind the complicated pattern that lead to his hand and fingers, that Al couldn't handle it anymore. The straps seemed to curl ominously. The young man had been instructing him with missionary zeal, but Al never actually heard what he'd said. At first he only muttered something about it being much later than he thought. Then he'd had to pull away the straps wrapped around his head.

"Claustrophobia," he'd said as a more-or-less polite excuse. Then he'd really panicked. How would he have answered his mother at this moment? She'd warned him enough times. Never be in a situation where you can't get out quickly. That's what had saved her.

So, when he couldn't easily unwind the complicated pattern around his arm, he'd started to claw at it. His young tutor had un-wrapped the mysterious-looking design quickly, handing back his jacket and opening the door, all in one smooth motion.

"Perhaps there are too many memories?" he'd asked. "Perhaps you would like to speak with…?"

But Al never heard the end of the young man's suggestion. Muttering something mostly incoherent about claustrophobia, and pointing to the low ceiling of the '*mitzvah* van' as his reason for leaving, Al had bolted before his tutor could finish speaking.

He'd have liked to gone back to the van to tell all of them that he wasn't Jewish, just curious. But he couldn't bring himself to do it. It was too dangerous. He avoided that part of The Loop for a long time after that and vowed that he would never again get mixed up with religious zealots of any persuasion.

CHAPTER SEVEN

The next day, Friday, when Al opened the door to the victim's hospital room he found two uncomfortable looking men where he had only expected one.

He'd already charmed the man's name out of a girl who worked at the hospital. That had only taken one phone call. Dave Razkowski sounded like a Polish name to him, not a Jewish one.

Al's source at the hospital had been quite helpful in response to his first, casual questions. "There's no profession listed on the admission form. But he does have medical insurance, some kind of plan that's offered through a sports association."

Then—people love to keep a celebrity talking—she'd volunteered some real information. "He's got a next of kin listed, Robin McDonald. That's R-O-B-I-N, just like the bird. And, would you believe it? Right now her name is posted with a Do Not Contact. That means his condition is stable enough so that he could direct the hospital not to call anyone unless his life is actually in danger. They have to comply, you know."

His informant's voice had taken on a cozy, gossipy quality. "I can't believe that he'll be out of here anytime soon though. He's pretty banged up. And you can't call his house, because that will get me in trouble. I shouldn't be doing this, not even for you."

She went on. "Probably they're divorced. That's usually why guys like this don't have a firm deadline to be somewhere, and why the woman has a different last name too. Or maybe the "Do Not Contact' order is because he hasn't figured out how to break the news that he's hurt."

Al would have liked more concrete information, like a phone number, but when he became more business-like his informant balked. "I think those questions are unethical," she'd said. He wondered if she had the attack of ethics before or after she'd realized that he wasn't interested in her personally.

"Thank you for all your help," Al had said, letting just an edge of sarcasm creep into his voice. He heard her voice rise as she tried to regain his attention. He'd said, "Gotta go," and hung up.

Dave Razkowski had come out of surgery armored in even more elaborate medical equipment than before. He wore a cervical collar that at least looked more comfortable then the first one. They'd re-bandaged his head, and put his right leg in traction. His torso, mid-chest to below his hips, was entombed in a white plaster cast so large it looked liked a chalk cliff.

Of course Al had checked with Minneapolis information. Razkowski had an unpublished number, and there was no separate listing for McDonald.

He didn't have to worry about 'Robin." The hospital would track her down. It seemed pretty likely that even if Razkowski thought he was some kind of Iron Man, he would be out of commission a lot longer than a few days. No one so badly injured mended in a day or two, no matter what prayers they said.

As Al entered the room he had read Razkowski's face like a book: pain, fear, and, at the same time, fury poorly restrained.

The second man in the room, obviously an Orthodox rabbi, seemed to be the object of his fury. Apparently Dave Razkowski didn't like religious types any more than Al.

"You can't keep me in this place," he shouted. "Are you going to tell me what the fuck you really want?" The words exploded out of Razkowski. Surprise made the rabbi's face a mask. Al understood his confusion. No Jew who said the *Sh'ma* would ever say something like that to a rabbi.

Razkowski strained against the medical equipment tethering him to the bed. He would have attacked had he been able to get free.

"Sie dreckiger Hund. Sei sind ein Schew." Just like on the tape. Al wished he understood. They'd been wrong not to let him learn any German. You had to know the language of your enemy.

Razkowski turned to Al. His eyes were a cool gray shade, but just now they blazed. Whatever drama was being played out, Al's entry into the room only stopped the patient momentarily. "I suppose you're going to tell me you're some kind of priest?"

Despite his fear, Al hung on to his protective credentials. "Mr. Razkowski," he said formally, despite his almost overwhelming desire to run. "I'm a reporter with...."

He'd hoped the exquisite tension in the hospital room would dissipate when he announced his profession, but it did not.

When Al's adrenaline started flowing he could always do several things simultaneously. This was just such a moment.

Mentally he set up camera angles, all the while watching the other two men. Their emotions rolled over him, as easy to understand as speech. Shock and anger from the rabbi and, despite his bravado, fear and anger from Razkowski too. Al knew fear when he saw it. Why would Razkowski be afraid of an Orthodox rabbi? Those people had never fought back.

This will be a terrible place to do television, he thought glancing around the small room. They were in the oldest part of the hospital, in a room with surprisingly dark, green-painted walls—a color from another era.

The camera work would have to be tight because the walls were so dark. The bed was old and banged up. It looked awful. At least a camera wouldn't record the rubbing alcohol and disinfectant smell of the place.

There were a few items on an off-kilter table that should have been over the bed: half a dozen daisies wrapped in cellophane and a loaf of bread in clear plastic. The braided bread, a *challah*, was traditional for the Jewish Sabbath.

Then, suddenly, from the corner of his eye Al saw the patient's left arm flash, as though he was trying to strike something. A loud clang followed, echoing in the small room. Amazing, but with only one free arm, Raz-kowski had managed to pick up the chrome spit basin beside him on the bed and launch it as a weapon. His awkward left-handed throw had managed to direct the missile toward the rabbi, clearly his target.

"They're coming," his mother's voice in his ears, and the shrieks and groans of his father's nightmares when he tried to sleep through the night. This was a moment his family had been preparing him for all his life. This man wanted to kill Jews. For a second only one thing reeled through Al's mind: his backpack of supplies, the things his mother always insisted had to be at hand, were stored in his apartment. He only had his wits and his work. And, he dare not turn and run.

Dave Razkowski had missed the rabbi, but there had been considerable force behind his throw. The edge of the small, chrome bowl had actually marred the old, green paint on the wall.

This lunatic probably wished that it had been a bullet.

The Rabbi recoiled, glaring at the patient and at Al as though they were in cahoots. Al couldn't even think about correcting that idea just then. He needed every ounce of his strength just to stand still. He waited through one heartbeat, then another. Then, with a magnificently casual gesture, he walked over, bent and picked up the small, shiny basin. He strolled over to the still-enraged patient.

Al knew his mother would have done the same, would have approved. He was getting it right. Her voice, 'they're coming' was playing at counterpoint against his own mantra: *He wants to kill Jews. If I run, I'm dead. He'll know I'm a Jew. I've got to go forward, placate him for now.*

"Good arm, considering," Al said. He was pulling it off, so casual, so friendly, as if he'd known Razkowski all this life.

"But it won't win your girl a panda bear," he continued, handing the spit basin back. "Care to try for two out of three? Or do you want to go for today's special on the clergy?"

The noise that came from Razkowski might have started as a laugh, but it emerged as a gasp of poorly suppressed pain.

"I just came to see how he was doing," the rabbi, the direct target of the anger, said. "I don't know what I did."

"You don't scare me. I've known worse," the patient snarled. At least now they were all speaking English.

"Worse than what? You almost died." Clearly the rabbi was confused as well as angry. He looked at the over-the-bed table, then at Al.

"A bread, *challah*, and flowers. Not for him. They are for other patients, for their Sabbath." He announced that to the whole room in a general kind of way, as though there were other witnesses.

Then, surprisingly, the rabbi's control vanished completely. He picked up the articles he had brought and stormed at Razkowski, his face contorted with anger as he shouted, "Are you crazy? Are you some kind of an anti-Semite, or just an animal? Why would I bring you flowers or *challah*? You would just take pitching practice with them! I told you. I am the one who spotted you in that *Gehenna*, that Hell, where you were obviously either trying to prove you are some kind of a man, or trying to commit suicide. Well, you failed. You're still alive, and you've only proved that you are a wild animal!"

The wide hospital-room door was rigged so that it couldn't slam despite the energy the Rabbi put into it. As he left, it swung slowly shut behind him.

His enraged speech and his manner of leaving the room momentarily held the attention of the two left there.

"The fuckers will get us all sooner or later," the patient muttered. He was pale, almost green, and sweat beaded his face.

Al pretended to consider the remark seriously. "Clergymen?"

"Jesus, you're a mealy-mouthed jerk. Who in the hell are you? I don't care what you did for a living. What difference does that make here?"

What was this man talking about? Where did he think they were?

Al only knew he had to stay with this lunatic, he needed to know as much as possible.

He had to ask one more question, to see if there was anything more to learn. "Do you mean all the Jews will get you?"

"In a place like this, what would it matter what I think about 'all the Jews?'" Razkowski's voice cracked, harsh, but shaky too.

Al had seen enough. Razkowski was obviously dangerous, even lying in bed and largely unable to move. Yet Al had trouble pulling himself away. Was this what his parents had felt, his grandmother too, in the presence of their enemy? His mind registered every image, analyzing, analyzing. The guy had to be in terrific pain. Hopefully, Razkowski had aggravated his injuries. He deserved pain. He probably deserved to die.

Al could also see that quite suddenly Razkowski was past being able to provide answers that would mean anything. His eyes only focused for a moment. His words came in gasps and spurts, his voice harsh, but shaky too. "Look, Not interested…right now…not even in Jews. Not clergymen. God Himself can't be in this place. You're useless…get the hell out!"

CHAPTER EIGHT

rateful to escape, Al left Razkowski's room. He didn't want him to die while he was anywhere nearby. As he passed the nurses' station he said in an off-hand way, "That guy in seven-twelve could use some assistance." It was best to appear casual. Who cared it that miserable anti-Semite had to wait.

Now Al had an urgent mission; he had to find the man who'd shared the last few minutes with him, as a fellow witness. As he passed one of the nurses he said, "I need to find that rabbi that was just here. Do you know where he's going next?"

"You want Chaplain Blumen?" she answered. Her smile made it clear she liked having a TV celebrity around.

"Blumen? He's the Chaplain? Yes. I need to find Blumen." Automatically he flashed one of his best professional smiles; he might need her for something later.

He had to pursue this story now, no matter the personal risk. He needed to confirm that Blumen had been the one to find Razkowski. He needed to know everything about Razkowski. He must be one of the crazies. There were dangerous groups all over the Dakotas, the real lunatic fringe. It seemed that with the turn of the millennium coming up in a few years those groups were getting crazier all the time. They hated everyone: blacks, Roman Catholics, immigrants. Especially, they hated Jews. He had to get out of South Dakota.

It took Al nearly an hour to catch up with Chaplain Blumen. By then he knew that his response wasn't personal. This might actually be an important national story. He would just stay cool and professional, detached. If the story really concerned anti-Semites he should cover it. The best protection always lay in controlling the story.

Maybe it would good enough to gain him the national attention he needed. If Razkowski was dangerous, it could even be the story to lift him out of Sioux Falls, away from KLON.

Al had trailed Blumen through several locations before he found him outside the parking garage. No matter how much Razkowski must have upset the chaplain he'd obviously fulfilled his professional duties. He'd visited several patients, so he no longer carried flowers or the braided bread. Like any executive, he seemed to be concluding his day by checking through the pages of a small pocket calendar.

The hospital's new parking garage had been constructed of dark gray concrete that managed to look already stained and still wet, all at the same time. The architect had tried to be creative in the design of the exit ramp. The corkscrew of concrete looked like it might unwind at any moment.

"Rabbi, Rabbi Blumen? I'm so glad I caught up with you."

"Look, I don't need you or your friend's curses," Blumen said, glaring. He was more than six feet tall, with a husky build, deep chest and long arms. Al, several inches shorter, felt slightly overwhelmed, but he pulled his role as a reporter around him like a cloak. That always felt safe.

"All you Jew-hating bastards will go too far one day," the rabbi continued. His wide-legged stance suggested that he'd been in a fight or two during his life and that he knew how to handle himself.

Al raised his hands. "Hold it! Hold it! I'm not his friend. I was just trying to find out something about him. I'm not one of them, not a hater. I really am a reporter. That's what I was trying to say when he blew up. Al Logan, Channel 7, KLON. You've probably seen me do the news."

"I'm not familiar with it. We only watch taped material at home."

But, even if that was true, he relaxed somewhat, although the expression on his face still telegraphed hostility. Obviously this man didn't let his guard down quickly.

Al tried to think of something to say that would relax Blumen further.

"I'd like to ask . . ."

His voice trailed way to silence. He couldn't think what to ask, even though he now had this man's attention. He certainly didn't want to come off as glib or superficial. He went with instinct. Defer for now; think about it all later. "But then I think I'm keeping you. It must almost be time for your Sabbath." It sounded lame, but at least it was safe.

Whether Blumen watched TV or not, his answer showed that he knew something about the media.

"Thank you. That's thoughtful. You must have deadlines. You have a story to write or broadcast. But, you also understand that it's almost the Sabbath. That's a point for you. Tomorrow night, call me. Then we'll talk."

He turned to enter the car park. Al stayed with him, just in case. It was the reasonable thing to do. Where else would his car be parked? He walked along side the chaplain, working hard at looking relaxed. His mind sped along so fast it was difficult to hang on to orderly thought.

Was this story really about a rabbi rescuing a professional anti-Semite? But, if Razkowski was an anti-Semite, why had he said the *Sh'ma*? What kind of perverted reason would a Jew-hater have for repeating that?

As those questions buzzed in his brain, Al realized one crucial thing. His private signal, one that told him he had a wonderful story, was washing over him. He hadn't felt the sensation in all his years at KLON; the sudden white-hot blaze behind his eyes, the almost sexual thrill racing through him.

Finally, he had the story he needed, and he had a journalist's greatest luxury: time. He could take the investigation of this story slowly.

Usually, he worked in a blaze of speed. Pulling back, moving slowly was actually more difficult. But, after four years he knew how rare a national story was in South Dakota.

The Chaplain stopped at a first-floor reserved parking spot. He drove a full-sized, dark blue panel truck that had been converted to a van for passengers. Children's car seats were scattered throughout the back rows. A beat-up blue and white sticker on the rear bumper said: "And on the seventh day He rested. Why don't you?"

A second sticker even older than the first one, said "Peace"' in a typeface that looked like Hebrew lettering. On the back window the newest message advised: "Rest by the Light of Sabbath Candles."

The driver side door displayed a magnetic sign that read 'The South Dakota *Mitzvah* Corps.'

Al stepped back, memories of that other *mitzvah* van alive again. He hoped it just looked as though he was making room for Blumen. The intense, bearded man didn't seem to notice anything unusual. He was a busy executive again. He fished in his jacket pocket and brought out a slightly dog-eared stack of business cards and headed one to Al.

"Call me after the Sabbath," he said, glancing out of the parking garage, toward the horizon, as though he had some responsibility or control over the passage of the sun.

"An hour and fifteen minutes after sunset you can call," he said. How could anyone, even a rabbi, believe that a dangerous world ran with that kind of precision?

Even if Blumen might turn out to be the hero of his story, Al felt hostile. His calm in the face of the encounter he'd just endured with Razkowski seemed like religious naiveté. He ought to see the threat in a man like Razkowski.

Blumen swung himself up into his truck as comfortably as any Dakota cowboy or rancher. He started the motor, revving it as though he drove a powerful sports car. He grinned. Al realized they were about the same age. The full beard and the side curls didn't disguise the Rabbi's unlined face and his clear, dark-brown eyes.

It was easy to believe that this man could pilot an airplane, save a life, subdue anyone who attacked his faith. Maybe that was why he'd become angry, but wasn't frightened. Or, maybe he was just good at hiding how he really felt. Maybe they shared that too.

Whatever Rabbi Blumen was thinking, his good-bye made one thing clear. His acceptance of Al was conditional.

"I hope what you do is important to you, and that you do it well," he said. If you're really one of the good guys, I'll know very soon. If you're not, I'll know that too."

Here was a man who obviously liked to make a dramatic impression. That was good. Al could always use that. Blumen must like good publicity too. Anyone with a cause liked publicity.

The Rabbi smiled once more at Al, his perfect white teeth glinting through his beard. Then he peeled considerable rubber as he pulled the van out of the parking ramp.

After Wolff Blumen left, Al headed toward the top floor of the parking structure to get his car. He walked slowly up the incline, making notes as he went. A dusty all-terrain vehicle drove past him and pulled into a slot with a 'reserved' sign. The Minnesota plates and a heavy coat of dust made it likely that he was looking at Dave Razkowski's Jeep. He knew that someone was supposed to drive it to Sioux Falls, but he was surprised that it had arrived so soon.

A very young man in a Park Ranger uniform got out.

"Nice," Al said, indicating the vehicle. "I've been thinking about getting one. How's the mileage?"

"It's not mine," the Ranger said, confirming Al's premise. "It belongs to a guy they rescued yesterday. It's great! I wouldn't mind having one myself."

"Yeah, it's real nice looking. Hope that guy appreciates the favor."

Al walked on, rounding the corner to the highest level of the parking garage. Then he waited, hidden, watching as the young Park Ranger walked away.

Al doubled back to the Jeep. He'd seen a green backpack taken off the rescue helicopter with Dave Razkowski, but there was no way he'd ever get access to that. What had the Ranger managed to salvage? And, there could be important evidence—books and pamphlets, maybe even hidden weapons—that Razkowski kept in his Jeep at all times!

He stood a moment by the dusty vehicle, considering the next step. Should he chance it? How big a risk? His mother's voice, usually so soft, repeating, "They're here. What will you do?" This was just like he was younger, doing something forbidden. What if they came just as he was breaking in to the car?

He shook away his mother's voice, and with that, fear. How could anyone ever know exactly what the kid had retrieved and what he had overlooked? If he used anything he found in the Jeep, he'd just claim that it had been sold to him or given to him.

There was no point ignoring the easiest and the most obvious ways to get into a car. First he tried the doors, but, as expected, the young Ranger had locked the vehicle up tight. Next the wheel wells. He found the magnetic box holding the key at his first try, rear tire on the driver's side. If anyone came, he'd just say... He wouldn't worry about that. He always thought of something.

There were very few cars left on the upper levels of the parking garage, but Al didn't want to linger. If someone challenged him, he could say the patient had asked him to look…

Once the Jeep was open a fast look inside told him there were no pamphlets or books. Fine, he'd settle for something that would make a good picture.

In the back of the Jeep he saw just what he wanted. A murderous looking climbing axe rested there, cold gleaming steel. It would make a great picture. His reward equaled the risk he'd just taken.

The kid who had brought in the car had obviously been told to revisit the site of Razkowski's fall. He had been thorough. Al saw cut away clothing and a slashed climbing boot too—just the kind of thing people would assume had been left behind. He took the boot. One boot, damaged that way, could have a certain pathetic quality. Or, it could even repulse an audience, which might be useful, depending on what he wanted them to think about Razkowski.

Al's fear had caught up with him by then. How could you tell excitement from terror? Like the motorcycle he'd bought when he'd first earned some of his own money in high school. It had been so exciting at first. Or maybe he couldn't discern the difference between excitement and fear even then. Certainly he'd come to hate and fear the bike. But, his family had hated it even more.

Logically, he knew that there was really very little real risk in what he was doing. He never took big risks. But, no matter, right now his heart hammered at his chest wall and his breath whistling in and out. He sounded just like his father, even if his lungs would never belch out that cigar-laded stink. How had his mother always kept her breathing so soft right through that dramatic whisper, "They're coming. They're coming." For just one moment it all seemed so real, as though it was happening again, that Al fumbled as he replaced the key. But he carefully put the magnetic box back before finally running to the safety of his car.

Over the years he'd learned that fear passed, panic receded. It was just the price you had to pay. Actually, it had gone as well as if fate had decreed it.

But, he had to sit in his own car a long while before he dared drive. By the time his fearful voices had stilled, he'd told himself that no one would care that he'd taken the boot or the axe. After all, he needed them to do the story properly.

As if to prove he was calm, he sat in his car working, turning it into his office. What better place, if they ever did come? He finished his notes, with a special reminder to let Blumen wait a little before he called. It didn't pay to let anyone else manage you too easily.

Finally, as the sun began to set, and the dome of the sky darkened, Al went back to his apartment.

CHAPTER NINE

When Dave didn't call by Friday, as he'd said he would, Robin knew that this time his trip had gone wrong. She was certain Dave had something to prove when he went away, but he was never deliberately cruel. If he'd said he'd call, he'd call, unless it wasn't possible.

Maybe he'd stayed out longer, because something hadn't been quite right. Ordinarily that would have infuriated her. Now she would have been relieved to know that was the reason for his silence.

She didn't worry that he had just deserted them. She'd known right from the beginning that Dave would always be honest and faithful. If he'd decided to leave he would have said so. Unfortunately, her certainty about that made it all the more likely that he'd been hurt.

There was no one Robin could share her thoughts with. There was no one at work. The only neighbors she and Dave knew slightly were the rabbi and her husband next door, Tovah Feldner and Dave Goldin.

She'd waved to Tovah that morning as the rabbi had left for services for the Temple where she worked. But Robin would never bother a casual neighbor with her concerns about Dave. Tovah and Dan had their only problems anyway. Their daughter, Leah, clearly had some sort of physical disability. She was past two but wasn't walking yet. Dan apparently managed her therapy, which was likely why he was the at-home parent.

Her worries about Dave should have prepared her for the Saturday afternoon phone call, but they didn't.

"Mrs. Razkowski?"

Obviously some sales call. "Robin McDonald," she snapped back.

"I'm calling regarding a Mr. David Razkowski."

"Yes," she said, a little unwillingly. "This is his home."

"Oh, right," the woman said. "It's Robin McDonald. I have that here. I'm calling from the Sioux Falls General Hospital. I'm afraid your husband has been in an accident."

The moment, that news, held Robin captive. She couldn't utter a word. She could barely inhale.

The voice on the phone had paused, but now it went on,

"Ms McDonald?"

Robin gasped out, "Yes."

"It was quite a serious accident, I'm afraid. He's had two surgeries and is unconscious right now. But he is alive. Believe me; his condition is actually quite good given the circumstances."

Robin's bright yellow, white, and blue kitchen had gone gray around her. Thank God Sunny was outside playing. She could listen to this news while she was alone. She almost fell onto the barstool next to the kitchen wall phone.

The voice in her ear tried to offer some support, but every sentence struck like a blow.

"It was a climbing accident. I'm the surgeon who operated, Katherine Haines. He's fractured several bones. He was reasonably stable, fully conscious the first day or two, but then he developed a hematoma, bleeding into his skull. He wouldn't let us call at first, and we had no choice but to honor that. He said he wasn't expected until the very end of the week at the earliest, that he didn't want to worry you unnecessarily. I don't know what he thought would be gained. But then we had to operate again yesterday, well, early this morning. We had to call, of course."

"What? Can I...can I come there?" She had to get to Dave.

"If you can manage it, that's what I'd recommend. There's always that risk with head and spine injuries."

"Both his head and spine? Is he paralyzed?"

But Robin didn't hear the doctor's answer. The noise of her own body roared in her ears, her heart pounded in her chest, drowning out the voice on the phone. She felt as though she'd been on a treadmill at an easy walk when somebody, without telling her, upped the pace to a dead run.

The rest of the phone call was even more of a blur. Her mind kept issuing orders at counterpoint to what the doctor was saying.

"If you let us know when you're arriving we'll have a chaplain meet you."

Call the boss. Call Sunny's school to tell them she'll be away.

"We have housing available for patients' families who come from a distance. Do you think you might have need of that?"

Tickets! Take the bus? No, that's too slow. I could drive. No. An airplane! That means I'm going to have to use the credit card.

"Will you let us know when you're arriving? And your husband's Jeep has been retrieved. We have it here."

I don't know if I can do this!

"Ms McDonald. Write this down. It's the number for the hospital. Please call us back when you've made your arrangements."

Robin realized that the phone was still in her hand, and that the caller was still talking to her.

"I'll be there. I have to...," She was crying. At the other end of the line the doctor waited for her to regain control.

Finally the doctor repeated, "Write this down. I'm Dr. Haines, Doctor Katherine Haines. Here's the number, the hospital's phone number."

"Two tickets to Sioux Falls, right away," she said firmly over the phone to North Central Airways.

There was only one flight a day on the weekend and she'd missed the one for Saturday, so she'd have to wait a whole day. She'd known the tickets would be expensive the way she bought them, one way, without any advance booking. Still, the price stunned her. More than she earned in a month.

CHAPTER TEN

By the time Wolff received the assignment to meet Dave Razkowski's wife and child at the airport he'd learned enough to be at peace with what had happened at the hospital on Friday afternoon.

He'd had a chance to talk to his father-in-law, too, telling him about the insight he had gained after spotting the climber. Despite the difficulties over their marriage, Wolff had the greatest respect for Rabbi Goldfein and still considered him his teacher.

The two men spoke at length after the Sabbath. Wolff had already shared the whole story with Faiga earlier in the day telling her what his reaction to saving the climber had been. He also told her everything that had happened in the hospital when he visited on Friday.

Faiga sat and listened as Wolff spoke to her father. When he hung up she smiled at him, looking very pleased. "That wasn't only about your climber, was it?" she said.

Wolff flushed like a child proud of an especially good report card. "No. He actually asked my advice about some of the newest students at the beginners' *Yeshiva*. Some of them have backgrounds like mine, not as performers, but as Holocaust survivors' children. He wanted to know what my thoughts were. He even said I had knowledge of the world that was useful, and that he would tell the *Rav* about our conversation. I don't think I've ever had a compliment like that from your father." Wolff looked very pleased, but a little confused, too. "He said such an odd thing when I told him about what I thought the rescue might mean."

"What was that?"

"He said he was happy to hear that I no longer believed in magic. And when I asked him what that meant, he said I should think about it, and, that we would talk about it again, soon."

At the airport Wolff stood holding a sign, the name "McDonald" printed out on a white board. But he didn't need it. There was only one young woman on board who had a child with her. Robin McDonald was a slim pretty woman in her thirties, with short blond hair. She was casually dressed in jeans and a light blue sweatshirt. She carried a leather jacket and had a knapsack slung over one shoulder. She was holding the hand of a little girl who wore pink jeans and a miniature pink and white version of a Boston Celtics jacket.

As always, not shaking hands was a little awkward, but he got around the moment by bending down to the child. "I have a little girl just about your age at home," he said, whereupon the child hid behind her mother.

"We didn't get this quite right," he said, smiling at his charges. My note says, "Robin McDonald and son."

"That's Sunny," she said, spelling the name for him. "And, I'm sorry. She'd usually not shy. She'd not used to…to…flying." Clearly she didn't want to say, "She's not used to men who look like you."

"And maybe not used to beards, either," he said, smiling again. The woman smiled back at him, but she looked around too, clearly anxious to be on her way. He led her through the crowd to the luggage carousel. It had been years since he'd paid any attention to the people who stared at him.

Robin wasn't surprised that people watched as the three of them waited for her luggage. Chaplain Blumen was a big man, at least six foot two. He had a long, square, untrimmed beard. He was wearing a black hat, a white shirt, a severe black suit with white fringes of some sort that came out over his belt and flapped against his trouser legs. He didn't seem to be at all self-conscious. He gave them his full attention, genuinely concerned for their welfare. Did Robin need a cup of coffee, or did Sunny want a drink before they went to the hospital?

"We can do all that later," Robin said.

The Chaplain's car was a big van, equipped with car seats for various sized children. Robin buckled Sunny into the proper booster. "She'll be asleep in a minute," she said over her shoulder. "She'll be frightened if she wakes up and thinks she's alone, so I'll sit back here where she can see me."

She was glad she didn't have to make too much small talk. She was worried that the chaplain would feel he had to stay with her every minute, even when she saw Dave for the first time. How could she concentrate on Dave and on how she should react in front of a stranger like this, all at the same time? All the way to the hospital she tried to think of a polite way to make him leave her alone with Dave. When they arrived at the hospital it was the chaplain who was all business. "We'll go to Intensive Care, and then I'll see what housing is available for you," he said as Robin carried Sunny, now sleeping soundly, into the hospital.

He moved toward her. Robin knew he only meant to help by offering to carry Sunny, but she found herself clutching at her child as though he meant to take her away.

Thankfully he understood and instead of trying to take Sunny, he pulled out the folding wheelchair stored near the hospital's front door. He pulled the chair open, adjusted the back to recline then gently rolled the chair toward her. She immediately deposited Sunny on the seat, covering her with her own jacket. She smiled at the Chaplain, this time with satisfaction at his neat solution to her problem.

He said, "You know, we could speed things up if you can go to Intensive Care by yourself. Since your daughter's asleep, and you have the chair, you could do that."

She grabbed at the opportunity.

"Thank you. That would be fine. I'll meet you back here in about a half-hour. I don't imagine they'll let me stay any longer than that."

"Nice to know when I'm superfluous," he'd said. She flushed pink, embarrassed that he'd figured out how eager she was to be rid of him. Obviously he wanted to put her at ease again because he said, "I'll meet you here at five-thirty. Intensive Care is that way, straight ahead. Just follow the blue line on the floor."

CHAPTER ELEVEN

"He's not quite as bad as he looks," one of the two nurses on duty told Robin. "Remember, he's had two surgeries and he got badly sunburned and dehydrated out there. Try not to see the equipment. Concentrate on your husband."

"I've never been in the hospital, except for when my daughter was born…and then only for…"

"I know, maternity, lots of life and love, not the same thing at all," the nurse said. With a glance toward her colleague, she stayed beside Robin, walking with her toward one side of the room.

There were eight beds in the area. Two were partly separated from the others by curtains that ran on tracks in the ceiling. The nurse stopped at the closest partially curtained bed. Robin felt as if she had walked a mile. She looked back toward the nurses' desk. The nurse on duty, along with Sunny sleeping in the wheelchair, seemed far away, pinpoints. She turned to continue the trip, then saw Dave's name mounted on the foot of the bed right next to where she stood. It didn't seem possible to be so close to him and not know it.

Her first impression was that there was no one in the bed. Rather, it seemed full of equipment and bandages. Resolutely, she looked past the traction equipment and the body cast. Then she almost wished she hadn't. The machines surrounding the bed didn't look nearly as bad as she'd thought they might. Dave looked worse.

He had scraped large areas of his face raw in the fall and the early signs of healing had made things look worse. There were scabby, brown crusts on his still-red face. He looked drawn and thin.

Most of Dave's normally long hair had been cut close, and part of his head had been shaved for surgery. She could see bare scalp where the awful-looking thing holding his head didn't cover completely. His scalp showed stark white. It looked dead.

She certainly couldn't pretend that he was just sleeping. Dave was a restless, energetic sleeper who tossed and turned constantly. "Like sleeping with a windmill," she told him. Now he lay stone still.

Very tentatively Robin approached the bed. She mustn't do anything stupid; the nurses were watching.

Fearful, she glanced back at the nurse who had accompanied her. There was only a look of concern on her face.

She took a deep breath and, as though reaching across a chasm, put out her hand to touch Dave's left hand.

Above his head, one machine traced an electronic, green, mountain-and-valley pattern that looked regular and strong. Beside it a number–77, 77, 77–blinked. That would be Dave's resting heart rate, high for him. He normally had the resting heart rate of an athlete, sixty or lower. Only one sound came to her ears, a regular, low 'beep, beep,' emanating from one of the machines.

She'd never thought that Dave could look so small and old. He was more than a dozen years older, but, until that minute, she had never considered what that might mean someday. Even if he lived through this he would die before she did. She would be left alone, just like she was alone now.

She gasped, and her knees buckled. She grabbed onto the side of the bed for support. The nurse immediately came up behind her.

Robin felt a chair pushed up. It touched the back of her knees and she let her legs fold. She leaned forward, bumping the bed slightly. The deathly still look on Dave's face altered a little.

"Can he feel pain?"

"Not likely. He's medicated for that," the nurse said. "But assume he can hear. You should assume that always. Don't talk about him as if he isn't here. Talk TO him."

She had to talk to Dave. That isn't hard. That's my job right now.

"Dave, honey," she said, "I took a plane. Sunny and I took a plane. We used the credit card and got two tickets. The first time Sunny ever flew. Only the second time for me, but I hardly noticed. I've been so worried."

Was she saying the right kind of thing? As she considered that and became self-conscious, her voice thinned out and disappeared. She looked back up at the nurse who gestured, a wave that said, go on, go on.

"People have been great," Robin started again. "The doctor who operated called me herself. Dr. Haines. We'll have to thank her. I'll have to thank her.

"I have to tell you what Sunny said one night. She wanted to show you her art from school, but of course you weren't there, so she said she'd leave it by the phone, in case you found a phone on the mountain."

She wanted to complete her little story by saying how cute that was. But when she tried to smile it turned into a grimace. The reality of Dave's condition rose up and shocked her into silence again.

To distract herself, Robin examined the traction mechanism as thoroughly as possible without actually touching it. Why the body cast?

She tried to imagine herself into Dave's body, to feel his injuries that way. She needed to know exactly what she and Dave were dealing with. Would the doctors tell her everything?

She looked all around and under the bed, too. He was immobilized in a half a dozen different ways. There was a bag collecting urine. That must attach to a tube leading right into his bladder. That made her skin crawl. In addition to everything else, Dave was receiving two different liquids intravenously. The clear plastic bags hung from a metal stand, attending him like a bodyguard. That wouldn't be just water they were filtering into his body. There had to be antibiotics and the pain medication too.

Dave would hate all this. He liked things all natural. He liked to be left alone.

She was trying to think of something more to say to him when one of the nurses came back.

"Robin," she said gently. "May I call you Robin? It's such a pretty name."

"Oh, please, yes." The nurses were already old friends in this frightening new world.

"You'll have to go, I'm afraid. You've already been here a half-hour. We ask visitors to leave during shift change at six. And, I think your little girl might be waking up. She'll be frightened."

Robin flew back to Sunny, relieved to have something to do away from Dave. Then she glanced back at him and felt guilty.

"I think I'll bring her to see him tomorrow," she said to the nurse. "She's so tired."

The nurse nodded agreement and handed her a tissue to dry her tears. Without knowing it, she was crying again.

She walked back to the bed and kissed Dave gently on the cheek. She patted his good hand. She only lost control for a second, long enough to grasp hard at his hand. There was no response.

She took one more look at the array of machines. The heart monitor now blinked 70, 70, 70. She felt some triumph over that. His lowered heart rate had to be a good sign.

"I'll be back early tomorrow, sweetheart," she told him, in the closest approximation to her normal tone of voice she could manage. She finished the thought in her head... *And they'll explain every last thing that they are doing to you, and what it all means.*

Robin took hold of the handles of the wheelchair, where Sunny still slept. She made sure she was standing perfectly straight, every inch of her five feet five inches erect, as though she was modeling perfect posture for one of her classes. Holding her head as high as possible, Robin marched back to the hospital entrance to meet Chaplain Blumen.

CHAPTER TWELVE

An apartment for you is no problem," Wolff Blumen said as Robin lifted Sunny back into the van. "You have a choice of a one or two bedroom. They're all the same, twin beds in each bedroom, a foldout sofa in the living room.

"As to payment, your insurance may cover some of the expense, or all, or you can talk to social services. You don't have to worry about that yet. The one bedroom is cheaper, of course."

"I'll take a one bedroom. That will be fine for us." Robin climbed into the van.

Just as the Chaplain started the motor and was about to pull out of the parking lot, Sunny woke up with a start and started to scream.

"Oh, this happens sometimes if she sleeps during the day," Robin said. Her face reddened with embarrassment.

Wolff wasn't perturbed. He raised his voice to be heard above the sound of Sunny wailing. "We've got one like this at home, my seven year old. He wakes up in a foul temper when he naps during the day."

They drove slowly through the somewhat shabby residential district near the hospital. Robin tried to soothe Sunny, but that made things worse.

Wolff pulled the van over to the curb, turning around in the front seat to face Robin. Robin caught a glance of her own face in the rear-view mirror, the rueful look of a parent whose child is out of control in front of strangers.

"It's not hard to imagine how she's feeling," he said. "How would it be of you come to our house? It's just around the corner. As a matter of fact, most of residential Sioux Falls is just around the corner. We can calm her down, let her move around a little and maybe feed her something. It's close to suppertime. You'll join us."

"Your wife won't mind if we just barge in at supper time with two more people to feed? I wouldn't want to impose."

Wolff had started up the van and was driving again, now with a clear goal in mind.

"She probably won't even notice two more. Eight or ten at the table, it doesn't make much difference."

She didn't really believe that Wolff Blumen and his wife had six children until the moment they were lined them up in front of her, by age, to be introduced.

Wolff began with his wife. Proudly he said, "Ms. McDonald, Robin, this is my wife, Faiga-Raisel."

Then he went on. "In order of age we have Shalom, Binyamin, Shayna and Moti. The babies are Yaakov and Aliza. Children, this is Ms. McDonald."

"You can just call me Faiga," Mrs. Blumen said with a smile. "It means a bird, so it's something like your name. Yours is prettier."

Faiga Blumen was the kind of person who provided answers, not questions.

"I bet you've just flown in," she said. "You must be exhausted. I'm sorry for your family's troubles. Shayna, why don't you show Sunny to the bathroom."

As the two little girls left the living room, Shayna glanced over at her brothers and said in a voice rich with experience, "We could really use another girl my age around here."

That gave the adults something to smile about.

Robin bent over and picked up one of the twins, the boy, Yaakov. At a gesture from her hostess she sat down in one of two wing chairs placed near an old blue metal school trunk that functioned as a table. Faiga had picked up Aliza and sat across from her, in the matching chair. The chaplain had disappeared, but now Robin saw him emerge from the kitchen carrying extra silverware and dishes to add to the already set dinner table. Robin let Yaakov explore her face with probing little fingers as she and her hostess smiled at each other.

Faiga Blumen started to nurse Aliza in a modest but matter-of-fact way. She seemed to be just a little older than Robin. The two women were the same height, with Faiga a little heavier than Robin. She had beautiful, soft, brown hair perfectly arranged in a pageboy, dark eyes, and a round, pretty face. She didn't apologize for her house, which was very plainly furnished and cluttered. Clearly the room where they sat served as living room, dining room and family room all at the same time.

The outside of the house had been very plain, too: a Cape Cod of white stucco with a red roof that came down low over a second floor just big enough for one or two bedrooms. In his winter contracting work, Dave was always dividing long narrow second floor bedrooms and adding extra bathrooms to Cape Cod homes.

Sunny and Shayna returned from the bathroom, already friendly. Shayna wore a long, dark denim skirt and a long-sleeved white blouse. Her dark socks disappeared under the skirt. Her outfit was nothing like what Robin would expect for a casual Sunday at home. The child's brown hair hung in two long braids. Her face was too mature for a little girl, its lines already sharp and defined. She might be a good-looking woman one day, but at the moment she was a somewhat plain, intense-looking little girl.

The Blumen boys were all dressed alike, in striped T-shirts and dark pants. Each one wore a skullcap. They also wore the same fringes as their father, which showed clearly against their dark trousers. Except for the very youngest boy, who had a full, tousled head of hair, they all had the identical haircut: Marine-short all over their heads, with a long side curl tumbling down each cheek.

The babies were dressed in perfectly ordinary terry stretch sleepers with attached feet.

A half-hour after they entered the little house they were all seated together at the Blumen's long dinner table, which stood at one end of the living room. Chaplain Blumen said grace in a strange language, then offered everyone bread.

Robin had a million questions in mind although what she actually said was innocuous.

"What beautiful soup." Tentatively she tasted it. "And it's delicious too."

It's just cold beet borscht," Faiga Blumen said. "It's very easy. It comes ready to eat in a big jar. To make it pink all you have to do is add sour cream and blend it in."

After the cold soup, Faiga served a noodle and cottage cheese hot-dish and fruit salad. The food was familiar enough to be comforting and exotic enough to be interesting.

By the time the children had eaten dessert and escaped upstairs to play, the adults had grown quite comfortable with each other. They sat around the table, finishing their meal with hot tea and homemade cookies.

"These are good. How do you find time to bake?" Robin asked. She had learned to keep house when she and Dave started living together, mostly by trial and error.

"Thank you again," Faiga said, smiling. "They're almost as easy as the soup. It's the only thing to do, here. Things like kosher cookies are too expensive to buy ready made."

Robin had only the faintest idea of what kosher meant. She thought it had something to do with pork. How it applied to chocolate chip peanut butter cookies she couldn't imagine.

When they had finished eating, Robin insisted on helping with the dishes.

"We don't usually let guests help, at least not the first time," Faiga said.

"Well, we can just imagine I've been here before." Robin said, stacking dirty dishes on the counter indicated to her.

There was a portable dishwasher in the corner, but Faiga didn't pull it out.

"I only use the dishwasher for meat dishes," she explained. "In a kosher home we separate the meat things and the milk things from each other, even in the dishwasher."

"And we just had milk," Robin said. Her hostess offered her a blue dishtowel then opened the kitchen cupboard where the dishes would be stored. There was blue vinyl tape on the edge of the shelf.

"Blue means milk," Faiga said. She started to wash the supper dishes in exactly the order that was taught in junior high home economics classes: glasses, dishes, silverware, finally the pots and pans. By the time they got to the last pan the two women were beyond small talk.

"Will your husband be in the hospital long?" Faiga asked.

"I think he will."

"What will you do with Sunny tomorrow? Will Wolff take both of you to the hospital?"

"He said he would, in the morning. He didn't seem to think taking the Jeep out tonight was a good idea."

"Oh, no, you wouldn't have wanted to do that in the dark and in a new place."

"Not to mention with a child who got hysterical."

"Well, she's fine now." They could hear the little girls playing in the living room. The boys were bounding around upstairs.

"That's called getting ready for bed," Faiga said wryly. "You know it would be just fine to bring Sunny here tomorrow. You might need to be at the hospital for a long stretch. Intensive care will be tedious for her."

"Would you baby sit her? It would be such a big help! I would pay you, of course. They said there's day care, but I think…I mean I had to take her out of kindergarten to come here."

"I suppose she could even go to kindergarten with Shayna. They can walk from here; it's just down the street. But I couldn't take money from you."

"Oh, but you'd have to. I'd have to pay for day care, you know. Just as you said, we may have to be here a long time. I don't know yet."

"Well, we could certainly give it a try for this week. Then if both of us are happy, we can make some arrangement."

Robin felt some weight lift from her shoulders. The necessities were addressed: an apartment, the car, and a baby-sitter. She'd even met this interesting and very friendly family.

Wolff looked in at the door of the kitchen. He had been running a vacuum over the dining area floor. "All done out here. Why don't we let the kids play for a while longer? Maybe just until the ceiling comes down," he said, gesturing over his head to the sounds of the boys' game. His simplest gestures were graceful, so at odds with the way he looked and the way he dressed.

"Once we have all the children totally exhausted I'll take you over to your apartment," he continued. "It's nice, please believe me. It's clean, fully equipped. It's even reasonably attractive. Tomorrow, I'll pick you up about nine thirty and take you to the hospital. I'll make sure you retrieve your car then."

The two women joined him in the living room. Robin knew the exhaustion she felt now was as much from her sense of relief as from anything else. It was hard to believe it was only seven-thirty.

CHAPTER THIRTEEN

When the doorbell rang right after dinner and clean up, it surprised all of them. Wolff went to answer the door. Clearly, another visitor was as unexpected as Robin and Sunny had been.

The Blumen's house had no vestibule or foyer, just a small, square space between the front door and the stairway to the second floor. Anyone entering the house was practically in the living room, so it was impossible for Robin and Faiga not to hear the conversation at the door.

The man at the door spoke to the Chaplain in a deep, powerful voice, a beautiful voice.

"Good evening, Rabbi. Do you know how our accident victim is today?"

"Ah, Mr. Logan." Blumen's response to his visitor seemed guarded to Robin, not at all what her welcome had been. She really wanted to hear the answer to the question that had just been asked. The man had referred to an accident victim, so they had to be talking about Dave.

"Mr. Razkowski will without a doubt be fine," Wolff Blumen said briefly, as if he wanted to leave the subject quickly. And, it's long after the Sabbath."

"Yes, I know," said his visitor. "I should have phoned yesterday. But, by the time it was okay to call it seemed very late. As for today, I often work all day Sunday. I put together the local magazine."

"TV, and a magazine too?"

"On-air magazine," the visitor said. That seemed a satisfactory answer, although Robin could see a slight frown on Faiga's face. She also thought that Wolff Blumen's posture suggested that he was less than happy about this visitor. Still, he gestured the man at the door all the way into the room.

The visitor was about five feet nine inches, and just a little chunky. He was also very handsome, with chiseled features, striking light-colored eyes, and brown hair cut so that the wave in it seemed to just balance, threatening to tumble down over his high, straight forehead. He was dressed in a perfectly executed version of the style Dave called 'casual decadence,' layers of expensive clothing: an elegant patterned sweater over a crisp white dress shirt open at the neck. His jacket, smooth, dark brown leather, matched his tasseled loafers. His freshly pressed jeans fit perfectly.

"Faiga, Robin, this is Mr. Al Logan. Mr. Logan, this is my wife, Faiga-Raisel, and a new friend, Robin McDonald."

Wolff continued, "Mr. Logan is the anchorman at a local TV station." Robin noticed that he did not mention her connection to Dave.

"Oh, you have company. I could come back," Al Logan said even as he continued to walk forward into the living room. Clearly he expected to stay. He practically bowed over each woman's hand, his smile pleasant and bland.

"Robin," he said, then, "Mrs. Blumen. Thank you for having me in your home."

CHAPTER FOURTEEN

"Shalom, will you do bedtime with the little ones tonight? Then you can come down for your own quiet time."

Shalom smiled conspiratorially at his father and hustled three of his younger siblings up the steep stairs opposite the front door.

Al had just settled in, hoping to sell Wolff Blumen on his idea of how dangerous David Razkowski really was. He'd hardly been able to be polite waiting to see if Faiga Blumen and Razkowski's blonde, Robin, would stick around. Fortunately, after a few minutes of polite conversation, a cup of tea and cookies, Blumen's wife had stood up and said, "You two men obviously have business. I'm going to take Robin and Sunny to their new apartment and help them get settled."

She had taken the keys she needed from her husband and shepherded Robin and her daughter out the door. Now, improving things even more, Wolff Blumen had sent the children upstairs under the supervision of his eldest son.

Turning the talk to the children seemed safe to Al. It would give him a few more minutes to think of how to direct Blumen to his way of thinking.

"Do bedtime? That's all there is to that? They're gone?"

"You seem relieved. Perhaps you should do a story about a household with six children? I certainly can't talk about patients."

"Fine looking, good looking kids. That might make a good story one day. And it's true; I'm not used to kids. So what about Razkowski's kid; his kid and his lady too?"

"His lady, as you so nicely put it, Robin, is off limits, too. I'm sorry. And certainly she had nothing to do with Razkowski's outburst. She has enough to deal with now. You will leave her alone please, just as you didn't bring up the subject of Dave Razkowski tonight."

Al's carefully constructed scenario, his plan for how this evening should proceed, crumbled around him. Blumen would not talk, and he wanted to be the one to set the rules of engagement. Well, nothing more would be lost by making a few vague promises.

"Just as you say," he said, as casually as possible. "But, suppose that little girl is being exposed to some kind of propaganda, or worse?"

"It doesn't seem much of a risk right now, and later we can see, if it still seems to be an issue. She seems a well-adjusted child. The mother is a good soul."

Al thought he knew something that would rile up a religious person.

"They're likely not married, you know. There's no record of a…"

"They live in the same house. They have a child. He mutters her name while in a coma. She comes immediately when he is hurt. That's plenty married."

"You surprise me, Rabbi. I wouldn't have thought you would be liberal in these matters."

"The issue is not liberal or not, or even religious or not. It is perhaps common law, and certainly common sense."

The way things were going, Al was relieved, although resentful too, when the Chaplain's interest shifted away from him again. The big man stood up and crossed the living room. He called Shalom's name up the stairs, listened for the response, and then asked a brief question in Hebrew.

"Are you asking him to rescue you?"

"No, I'm asking if the children have said their prayers. They'll listen to anyone read a story, but sometimes they'll balk at prayers with anybody but their mother or me. As if we are an official listening post. It is better they understand we are not. Their brother as the one in charge is still a novelty to them. Sometime it works, sometimes not."

"Now I lay me...?" Al recited singsong style.

"No. Just the one God," he said, holding up one finger, "and a prayer to the angels."

"Jews have angels?" Al asked. He knew the answer, but it was something to throw Blumen off his real identity.

"You would call them angels...and archangels. In the morning and at night the children pray for protection, to Gabriel, Raphael, Michael and Uriel. It's metaphoric perhaps, but also literal. They are protection ahead and behind, left and right. And above..." He ended with a gesture that suggested flight toward the heavens, or at least toward the ceiling of his home. "God completes it all."

"We sure don't forget the things we learned as a child, do we?" In his head Al followed along, words he hadn't heard in years. His father had insisted that the children learn the basics of Judaism at Sunday school, even though he never went to synagogue himself. Anatoly Lowenthal had finished with God after the concentration camps. Oddly enough, he didn't see any inconsistency in demanding that his children learn about their religion. Al had finished with it formally at the age of thirteen, although he'd learned a lot more since then with his obsessive reading. Not that he had a real *bar mitzvah*. His father had said that they weren't necessary. You turned thirteen; you were a *bar mitzvah*. The few thirteen year olds in Auschwitz, those who survived, they were *bar mitzvah* when they came out, with no fuss in synagogue, no party.

Wolff Blumen didn't respond the way Al would have expected. Instead he looked surprised. "I didn't know these things as a child. My parents did not believe. I wasn't raised to do any of this. The Judaism of my childhood was political, if it was anything. 'Incidental' might be an even better word."

"That's very interesting. How would you describe 'political' in that context?" He was reaching, trying to keep the conversation going. There would be no story if he couldn't get Blumen to talk. Maybe memories about his childhood would spark something. Thinking about his own childhood always spooked Al.

Shalom pounded down the bare wooden stairs then, generating the amount of noise only a small boy can produce. He was carrying a video tape.

Al had a few more moments to think while Wolf concentrated on his son. "*Sha, sha.* You'll wake up the dead—God forbid—not only the babies."

"*Abba*, the teacher told us to watch this tape before school in the morning, for history. I forgot before."

"Of course, you forgot." Wolff looked at his wristwatch.

"So, you have a barely a half an hour before bed. Is that enough time? And your mother will not be happy. She'll say you'll have nightmares, or not sleep at all."

"I won't have nightmares." Shalom shrugged off his mother's concerns.

As he spoke, the boy swiveled the TV partway around on its portable base, away from where the two men sat, as if the action created a separate room. He popped his tape into the VCR, then punched the buttons with the kind of expertise no adult could ever have.

Shalom rolled a navy blue beanbag chair from a corner of the room over to a spot in front of the TV, then folded himself into the chair in a way that suggested that he, like the chair, had no internal support structure at all.

"I used to be able to do that," Al commented ruefully. A dismal thought ran through his mind. There'd been one chance in a thousand that he could get out of town on the strength of the Razkowski story, and he could feel even that small chance evaporating.

His wry comment didn't get Blumen's attention anyway. For the moment Al could only sit there, watching. If he couldn't even get Wolff Blumen's attention, how could he ever convince him of anything? This man wasn't even willing to let his kid watch a damn videotape without supervision. He had left Al, his guest, completely alone, and gone over to squat behind his son, one hand on the boy's shoulder.

My brother Sandy would sometimes touch me like that, check up on me like that. My father never did.

Sandy, really Sandor, was sixteen years older, much more a parent than his father. Anatoly Lowenthal would never have worried about what was on TV. With his gasping breath and his shaking, old man tobacco-stained hands, he only had enough energy for work. Work was the most important thing in life, the only thing.

Now a smooth professional voice, very much like Al's own voice, emerged from the little TV. But it wasn't saying anything bland or beautiful…

As early as 1933, the Jews of German began experiencing…"

Al sat bolt upright, as though an electric charge had run through him. Wolff, his eyes on the TV screen his son was watching, didn't notice.

Even Sandy wasn't interested in me that day. We'd all been sent home from school. He and Victoria were home too, because even the University had been closed. President Kennedy had been shot. That day, Sandy didn't want to play. He'd taken me by the shoulders and spun me around, as though I was a soldier, so we were all facing our mother.

"Ma," Sandy had said, "Yes, the president's been shot. But no one will bomb us. There won't be a war."

His mother had given her eldest son a withering look, as though she had birthed an idiot.

"Children, it's time. They'll be coming any minute."

Victoria had started to cry. "No one is coming. They don't bomb people here. They don't have wars! They don't, they don't!"

Heddy had walked over to Victoria. Now Al realized that most people would have expected her to put her arm round her hysterical daughter, to try calm and comfort her. No one in his family had expected that.

Heddy had slapped Victoria, just once, across the face. "Stop," she'd ordered. The tears on Victoria's face disappeared as though from the heat of the slap or her reddened cheek.

He remembered every word his mother had said that day and in the days that followed. It was as though he'd gone to war with her.

She'd said, "It has happened. The communists have killed the president. The government here will bomb the communists and then they will come in retaliation. This city, Boston, his home, will be first"

For the Jews in Europe the Nuremberg laws were only the first step.

Al couldn't listen to a word of the video one more second; even if it seemed to hold the complete attention of both of the Blumens, father and son.

All that day Al had been reading through his secret collection of Holocaust literature, figuring out what to say to Blumen to convince him that Dave Razkowski was a dangerous neo-Nazi. He could not bear another moment.

He got up, unsure whether he should run or try to put a stop to words on television.

That day at home in 1963, even though he'd been so young, he'd known exactly what to do, what to expect, when he saw what his mother had arranged in the foyer. There were eight sets of backpacks, boots and coats, one for each person. They were lined up by order of age.

Why did I always have to go first?

Later his mother had admitted they'd all done well, better than usual.

Al had absorbed every word he'd heard. Walter Cronkite saying Lee Harvey Oswald had done it alone.

His mother didn't really care what the American media said. She didn't trust American television, and only thought some of the European short wave radio broadcasts might tell the truth. How had she known? Now Al also knew that TV news was mostly about entertainment.

His mother only cared about saving her family. All during those three days she said we were perfect, like soldiers, following orders, lining up, keeping track of our things at all time. Al had been the best of all, she'd said. Sometimes when he'd been really little and his mother had whispered, "They're coming" in his ear, he'd wet his pants. But he'd never done it from that day forward, not ever since November 22, 1963.

"The Nazi scourge would eventually envelope all of Europe and kill…"

He rushed toward the TV to turn it off, to stop it.

No more!

His foot caught on a chair leg and he stumbled. For a second it must have looked as though he was going to fall on top of Shalom.

Wolff Blumen made a desperate grab for him, as though that was the worst thing that could happen to a kid.

Al regained his footing on his own. "You let me watch this…this obscenity?" He had to block the too-familiar story that smooth professional voice was recounting. .

Eventually six million Jews would die, along with many…

What did that numbers mean on its own? It had to mean more that some had survived. His mother had survived alone in Budapest. His grandmother and his father had survived the worst death camp of all, Auschwitz. His mother had been a hero, in Hungary and at home, saving herself, and later under the Communists, always protecting her family. They never got her. She could survive anything. She'd taught her children the same.

Al realized that he and Wolff were standing together now, wordlessly watching the television. Momentarily, Shalom had gone from watching the screen to watching them, gnawing on the tough skin on the side of his thumbnail as he did.

On the screen a silent parade of photos flashed by, rows and war of pre-War snapshots, small black and white pictures.

Most of the photos at home were just like that. Had anyone before the war ever been young? Even in the pictures taken at picnics and on ski trips everyone was so stiff, all the faces so formal.

The pictures were only different if his mother was in them, because she was so beautiful. Her beauty must have helped her survive.

But he couldn't think about that now. He still had to silence the videotape, turn off the pictures.

"You let him watch this…garbage?" Al asked, in desperation. Even though Wolff Blumen understood people so well, Al couldn't hide his feelings.

He knew right away that he'd done what his mother told him he must never do; he'd let someone know what he was feeling.

Wolff Blumen, damn him, understood much more than just the words Al spoke.

"It is his family history," the big man said mildly. The hand he'd put out to break Al's fall still held him tightly.

The big, bearded man finally loosened his grip just a little, but did not let go entirely. "His is the Polish part of the family," he said.

An odd thrill coursed through Al. They shared that.

"It's my history too." He had to say it; the words were wrenched from his mouth before he knew it.

The two of them stood watching the screen. It seemed somehow bearable, for another moment anyway. On screen youngsters not much older than Shalom, Brown Shirts, splashed paint around as though it was a weapon. To Al – and probably to the others watching with him – that paint still gleamed wet, red as blood. *"JUDEN RAUS"* "Jews Get Out." The three of them saw other Nazi vandals pulling books and *Torah* scrolls from the arms of bearded old men who tried desperately to protect the holy objects.

How could Wolff Blumen expose himself the way he did? He looked just like the old men on the screen, the same black clothes and the same kind of beard. Couldn't he see the danger?

Unwillingly, but unable to stop himself, Al finished what he'd started to say. "It's my family too, the Hungarian branch."

CHAPTER FIFTEEN

A little more than an hour after she'd left, Faiga came home so happy that she almost danced up the stairs to her front door. She felt wonderful, rejuvenated. Robin was a delight. She'd pretty much agreed to care for Sunny. She was amused by the fact that Robin had entered her life unexpectedly, as had Wolff, over a casual family meal, someone brought home by the performance of a *mitzvah*.

If her father had known that bringing Wolff — still William then – into their home would end with marriage, he'd have left Wolff where he'd found them. He wouldn't have concerned himself even though William Flowers was a Jew, even though it was obvious to her father that he was suicidal.

The house had a closed, shuttered look even though it couldn't be much later than nine o'clock and though Al Logan's TV station car was still parked in the street. Not wanting to disturb the men Faiga restrained her delight, quietly letting herself in with her key.

Wolff had all the children in their rooms. He and Al Logan sat at one end of the long dining table directly across from each other. Only one small light was on over the table, so that darkness surrounded the two men like a wall. From Faiga's vantage point, the two men looked as if they were in a play on stage.

She stood at the front door long enough for Wolff to realize that she'd come home. Once she'd seen the flicker of acknowledgement in his eyes, she checked on the babies in their tiny nursery and then went to the bedroom.

Before she left the front doorway she saw that a fresh pot of tea sat on the table between the two men. The spout of the teapot steamed gently but visibly; they had obviously just settled themselves. The few cookies not eaten at dinner were on a plate. Faiga reminded herself to bake again in the morning. Sunny would be with them during the day.

As she prepared for bed she could hear the voices of the two men in the living room humming on together. Al Logan had a beautiful voice. He seemed to speak most of the time, with Wolff only responding occasionally. Wolff's voice was beautiful too. There was a lovely sound to their conversation, like music or song. It reminded Faiga of the sound of men praying, masculine voices entwined, floating up past the women's section on the upper level of the synagogue she had attended all her life in New York. She hoped that whatever Al Logan and Wolff were discussing was as beautiful as their voices.

PART TWO

Isaac: My father used to teach me many things
so I could learn to be a great chieftain, but since we
went up on the mountain, he is quiet and gentle and
only tells me that as I grow older, I, too, will speak
with God. When I wander in the fields at eventide
and sometimes watch a caravan pass by, I think
about my father finding the ram and wonder what
God will require of me.

from *Abraham and Isaac*
By Ruth Brin, on *Genesis 22*

CHAPTER SIXTEEN

During the days Dave was in Intensive Care, Robin discovered that the place was rarely calm or quiet. It had only been that way on her first visit, a nurse explained, because on Sundays only essential treatments were performed.

On regular weekdays the families of the patients were constantly arriving and departing. The ICU never seemed dim, silent, or sleepy.

The walls bristling with spigots and equipment holders pushed in on Robin. The area boiled with doctors and nurses who spoke in loud, flat voices. Each technician arrived accompanied by a distinctive sound. Those from the blood lab carried a tray that chimed with test tubes and syringes. For any EEG, EKG, x-ray or sonar imaging procedure, a huge machine would be trundled in, always on squeaky wheels.

The worst sound was the noise of the patients' metal-backed charts being hooked back on to the foot of a bed or slammed back into the case that held them between procedures. That noise was as awful as any fingernails-on-a-blackboard screech Robin had ever endured.

She spent a good deal of her time in ICU getting out of the way. A string of specialists flowed past her, each one wanting to check something or other, always unspecified. They would put a hand on Dave's blanketed figure as though they owned him, and indicate that they were going to peel back the blanket and do something horribly personal, or painful, or distasteful.

"If you'll just excuse us for a minute," they all said. Their manner indicated that she wouldn't want to view or even know what they were going to do to Dave.

Immediately following each episode Robin swore she would not let herself be spooked by the next expert. But she always was.

Beside the specialists there was Al Logan to deal with. Why did he want to know so much about Dave? He pretended to be friendly, wanting to buy her coffee or lunch. She would have liked to refuse. She'd spent too much time with men like Al Logan, men who thought they were doing you a favor if they paid you any attention. Dave had rescued her from the Al Logans of the world.

The day after she met Al at the Blumens he came by the hospital to visit. She refused his offer for lunch, but by three o'clock, when Dave hadn't moved all day, when his eyelids had barely flickered in response to her voice, she was desperate. Coffee with the TV anchorman almost began to look like an attractive option.

"So, let's talk," he said, imitating Joan Rivers. "Tell me about yourself. Where did you go to school?"

The comprehensive high school in Bemidji, Minnesota, the place where they'd lived when Robin had finally decided to leave her mother's quest for the next guy to support her, flashed through her mind. She'd finished twelfth grade there, even if she was only seventeen. And she'd earned an aerobics accreditation at the YWCA by then too. She was proud of the fact she'd been able to support herself at that age. But she ducked Al's question because she was pretty sure he had something more Ivy League in mind when he asked about school.

She couldn't quite bring herself to be rude to Logan, so it became essential to think of ways to duck his questions. Even if she'd been prepared to tell him everything, the truth was she didn't know the answers.

"So, what has Dave's family had to say about this accident?" Al asked. He followed up by wanting to know when they would be visiting.

It was clear the newsman wasn't amused when she told him what Sunny had said the first time she'd seen Dave, in answer to his question about family.

Robin couldn't bring herself to start a job hunt during those days. In fact, she couldn't do anything but drop Sunny off at the Blumens in the morning and hurry to the hospital. Dave might wake up any minute or, worse, he might simply continue to lie there. Either way, she had to be beside him.

Then, late on the fifth day of watching Dave lie so unnaturally still, Robin looked away for a moment to respond to a casual remark from one of the nurses. When she looked back, Dave was awake. He smiled.

"Hi, sweetheart," he said. "What's going on here? And where is 'here?'"

Once Dave had regained consciousness there were moments when Robin felt as though she was a character in some movie where an accident victim wakes up and has been possessed by some strange new personality.

No, that was too extreme. Dave was still Dave, but it was as if he'd had a whole secret life before, and now, probably because he had no choice, he'd suddenly decided to let Robin know all about it.

She'd expected to find she had an angry, restless man on her hands, a difficult and demanding patient. Instead Dave seemed almost relaxed, channeling whatever irritation he felt, even his pain, into a series of business calls that were totally mysterious to Robin.

She tried not to listen as Dave spoke to his accountant, his stockbroker, and even to a banker. All of these people seemed to take Dave and his assets–that was the word Robin heard over and over again, 'assets'–very seriously.

Robin had never heard of any assets before, beyond their house, and she'd had the impression that buying that had been a financial stretch for Dave. Otherwise, why would he have put so much energy into a 'fixer-upper' that had taken months of work? She didn't think the checking account she used and the credit card Dave had given her for emergency use—the card she'd used to purchase the airplane tickets—constituted assets. Now Dave talked about stocks and bonds that had to be monitored, monies that had to be managed. There were also insurance policies on which claims had to be filed.

There were no lingering moments of confusion for Dave. By the first evening they had removed all of his IV's. The next morning, at his request, Dr Haines approved a move out of ICU to a small private room with a telephone. There was no reason to keep him in ICU, the doctors told Robin. Not only was Dave fully coherent, he was taking much less pain medication then they would have expected.

Robin could believe that. There was nothing fuzzy about Dave's thinking. By the time she'd dropped Sunny at the Blumen's and arrived at his bedside that morning, he'd started on his business calls. Before the accident he must have done the same kind of thing in the privacy of his third floor office at home.

"Okay, okay," Dave was saying. "You need the papers signed. But I need the cash and I need it now. I have bills to pay. I've got my family here, but the mortgage goes on in Minneapolis. Why do you think I bought the damn insurance? Didn't the paper work get done then?"

"Dave, I thought I'd get a job here." Robin tried to whisper quietly.

"There, did you hear that, Jess?" Dave asked, interpolating Robin's whisper into the conversation. At the time she still didn't know that Jess was Dave's accountant.

"Here's my wife, with a banged up guy to worry about, and our daughter here too, and she talking about getting a job. She knows we need cash now, even if you don't."

My wife? Did Dave always talk about her like that?

After a few days Robin knew all of Dave's callers. Jess Lansdowne, the accountant, called most frequently. Arthur, Dave's stockbroker, called every day around the time of the opening and closing of the market. There was even a bank vice president who called.

Robin found herself trying not to pay attention to the calls, telling herself that they were none of her business. But it wasn't possible not to hear, not to feel that the conversations were very much her business. Dave spent a good deal of his time talking about her and Sunny.

Despite how uncomfortable she was listening to Dave's phone calls, Robin stayed close. He certainly needed her help with his meals and he seemed to prefer that she help him clean up in the morning. Occasionally during one of the calls Robin would find Dave's eyes on her, as though he expected her to ask a question.

Dr. Haines was the one who dared to ask questions. Why had Dave been climbing alone? Why hadn't he arranged a pick up? Why had he not taken more precautions, been in better contact with the outside world during his climb? The doctor tried all her questions out on Dave first. She didn't get any real answers beyond Dave's insistence that he didn't remember anything. The doctor then repeated her questions to Robin, but didn't like her answers any better.

They wouldn't be able to duck those questions forever. It appeared that the State of South Dakota, having rescued someone, wanted to know why the rescue had been necessary. Robin couldn't shield Dave from those questions. Nor did she really want to. She'd have liked to hear the answers to those questions too.

On the third day he was awake, Dave took one action that Robin silently applauded. Right after lunch Dave banished Al Logan from his room. He might only have had words to rely on, but he managed a full dismissal.

Al had brought a camera crew to the ICU the instant he'd heard Dave was awake. He did it without asking, assuming he had access. He got a short interview with Robin, an even shorter one with Dave, and a film clip of Sunny sitting on Dave's bed, creating her first crayon picture on his cast.

Once Dave was out of ICU, Al had continued to drop in. After his morning news shift he seemed quite willing to spend time sitting beside Dave's bed, chatting, falling silent whenever Dave's telephone rang, obviously prepared to wait and to listen, as Dave conducted business.

But Dave didn't think Al Logan had done anything to earn access, or any special privileges. He certainly wouldn't allow him to sit in his room listening to his phone calls. Wolff Blumen might have some rights of that nature, Dave said, but the chaplain didn't claim any. He just tried to help the whole family.

Finally Dave said to Al, "Logan, I'm sorry, but you're going to have to get lost. We've got a lot of work to do here."

The newsman flushed – only momentarily – as if he could control his own involuntary responses. He got up from his chair slowly, stretching elaborately, as though he'd only been sitting there because he thought Dave might need him. It seemed to Robin that she'd seen a flash of anger at the same moment Al's color had heightened, but it had only been for a moment. No matter what she was thinking, she didn't say a word. She just stood beside Dave, in the shadow of various pieces of medical equipment. It was ludicrous, but now that Dave had awakened Robin felt safe. It didn't matter that he was flat on his back and immobilized by injuries.

At the same time as Dave had lain in coma, something in Robin had awakened. Now there was that nagging internal voice she'd occasionally heard before, but always managed to squelch.

Before she'd always told herself that she, and by extension Sunny, were only in Dave's life as long as he wanted them. They had no claim on him, or on his possessions. Somehow she didn't quite believe that any-more, although she couldn't have articulated what she did believe. What was becoming clear to her was that the obligation between her and Dave ran both ways.

Dave seemed to delight in showing her off. He told every doctor and therapists who came by to consult on his long-term care, that Robin was his 'secret weapon.' She'd make it possible for him to go home much earlier than they planned, he said.

"She's an aerobics instructor," Dave said several times. "She knows every bone and muscle in the body, and what to do with it. And, we have a neighbor who has a daughter with Cerebral Palsy. He'll help too. You get me up out of this bed into a wheel chair, and I can go home."

The doctor's weren't quite as confident as Dave, but many of them took Dave's claim seriously enough to question Robin about her ability to manage Dave's physical therapy. They actually seemed satisfied that she'd be able to do the job.

"I'll have to get one of my crews in to build a temporary ramp to the front door," Dave told Robin. "We can put me to bed in the family room or living room for as long as necessary. I'm going to be just fine, you'll see."

Robin was left with too many unstated question for her own comfort. Why had Al Logan insisted that he and Dave had met and talked before Robin ever reached Sioux Falls? He wasn't just referring to when he'd initially covered the story, when the rescue helicopter had brought Dave to the hospital, but to some time between Dave's first and second operations.

Dave totally denied knowing Al Logan before he regained consciousness in ICU. He said he didn't care what anyone else claimed; he didn't remember anything until he woke up after his second surgery, unaware of where he was, with Robin sitting beside him. Robin preferred not to believe Al, because Wolff Blumen, who came and visited Dave regularly, never said a single word about an earlier meeting

Then, toward the end of the second week of Dave's recovery he gave her a wonderful excuse to go off by herself and think things through. One morning he handed her a pad of paper. "You'd better take some notes," he said. "You're certainly the only one I trust. You're going to have to go back to Minneapolis this weekend. Just for a day or two. It appears that I must have my insurance policies, and that you need to sign a bunch of papers for payments to begin. Remember, you signed some of the applications. You're the owner of some of the policies. You know how it is."

Robin had no idea how it was, although she had signed a lot of papers when they'd moved into the house. Obviously, Dave thought she'd understood exactly what she'd signed. Right now she wasn't going to tell him otherwise.

When they had moved to Minneapolis from Fargo she'd been so grateful that Dave had wanted her along, she certainly hadn't thought of negotiating terms or questioning anything he'd wanted her to do.

She couldn't share any of this with Dave. Her usual silence protected both of them from awkward questions, although it didn't protect her from some very uncomfortable feelings.

It seemed unreasonable to be angry with Dave, although she had to admit that reason didn't change how she felt. Why hadn't he told her about all of this a long time ago? Then too, why hadn't she asked?

She didn't have to fend of Al Logan's questions anymore and she was grateful for that. She didn't have to rush out to get a job; there was enough money because of Dave's preparations. She ought to be grateful for that too.

But, if there had always been enough money for insurance policies and expensive professionals like accountants, why had Dave let her worry over how little she earned? He'd never said there was any money beyond her small salary and what he made as a camping guide in the summer and as a contractor in the winter.

Over and over again, Robin told herself that Dave had never had to tell her anything; that she had never asked. More and more she realized that she wasn't convinced by the excuses she made for him.

So Robin was relieved to be leaving for Minneapolis on Sunday morning, even if those feelings upset her. She told herself it would be better when she got back, because she would miss Sunny and Dave while she was away. Fortunately, Dave didn't seem to notice her restraint when she kissed him lightly and said good-bye.

She left with a list of files to retrieve from Dave's office. She had an appointment to meet with Jess Lansdowne to sign papers. And some where, some how, she had to get rid of her anger. She didn't know which was worse: the anger she felt because Dave had withheld so much, or her fury at herself, because she had behaved like a ninny?

CHAPTER SEVENTEEN

Al told himself he was relieved to be free of Razkowski's hospital room. While Dave had been out cold in Intensive Care, he'd had time to work on Robin. But, like sitting in the hospital room, it had been a waste of time. Razkowski had obviously trained Robin not to talk.

Al hated hospitals. For his own surgery he had avoided regular hospitals and general anesthetic. No one was ever going to put him out cold.

He'd had his surgery in Mexico, careful about which clinic he chose, making sure it was a facility that only did celebrity work. Even then the place had turned out to be a hospital in disguise. It had oxygen ports and other emergency equipment hidden in the walls, even in the special suites where you stayed until you could go out into the world again. Many parts of the clinic had smelled the same as Sioux Falls General, antiseptic and cleaning solutions overlaying the odor of medicine and bodies.

Of course anything was better than the smell at home, his father's cigars. Did burning tobacco cover up the memory of burning bodies, and the other awful odors of the camp hospital where his father and his grandmother had managed to survive. No one at home would ever talk about what had happened there.

The cigar smell never seemed to bother either his grandmother or his father. It permeated everything in the house, especially in the office where both of them spent hours every day working on the books of their businesses, the barbershop, the hair salon and the cleaning company that Al had named, Steri-Clean. He could tell that the smell bothered his mother. She held her breath the few times she kissed her husband.

You had to have something to show for spending time in any hospital, something big like surviving, or something like the results of his surgery.

Few women had ever said no to Al, even before the surgery. So why should Razkowski's blonde, Robin, get away with keeping secret?

From the moment he met Robin at the Blumen's, he'd been so sympathetic, making a special point to see her every day, trying to arrive at times when he could buy her a cup of coffee, or suggest they have lunch together.

But the only place she'd consider going for lunch was the hospital cafeteria where the food looked like the same slop they served the patients.

The doctor's who ate there must come straight from their patients and out of the operating rooms. Most of them were still in their scrubs, some with clamps and other equipment clipped to their clothing.

They took more care in Mexico. The director of the clinic, and the chief surgeon, both in dark suits, white shirts, and elegant ties, had met with him first in an impeccably appointed boardroom. They were all ready with a computer generated 'show and tell,' which impressed Al, although he'd said, "Don't bother me with your computer-generated crap."

He'd pulled out the pictures he'd brought along, most of them taken in Hungary soon after the War. His mother would be his model for surgery.

The surgeon who did the work had been a European immigrant too. He'd understood immediately. "This is the real thing," he said, tapping a 1947 portrait of Mr. and Mrs. Anatoly Lowenthal with light, sensitive fingers.

"This is authentic, classical. Not the current nose, the way they want lips this moment, the boobies in this year's size. This is beauty." He peered closely at the picture of Heddy then peered at Al.

"Yes, not so much to do, really. Most people would be satisfied with the way you look now, very much like your mother. The chin, the nose–maybe a little more for a man–but even the cheekbones are basically there."

Then he'd indicated the wedding picture again.

"I can see, you and your mother both come by your good looks, by these wonderful bones, honestly."

With even more respect than before, as a connoisseur unwilling to bruise such a person–or even the picture of such a person–the doctor had gestured toward Al's grandmother, also in the photo.

Al had never paid any attention to Irene who was always in the family pictures. She was even in the wedding portrait, already elderly as far as he could see. Her face was toward the camera, but her eyes looked to one side, at her daughter and her son-in-law.

Al hadn't wanted to change his looks too much with surgery, and he got exactly that result. The Sioux Falls station manager who hired him barely noticed the change when he reported to work. Although, without knowing it, his new boss did note the improvement. He'd said, "Did you lose a few pounds or something? Amazing what a little vacation between jobs can do. Anyway, you look great, better than ever. Get some new publicity pictures."

Al hadn't been able to count on his celebrity or looks to impress Robin. Maybe she wasn't bright enough?

He tried to be really nice, but that didn't work either. He could sense her stiffening every time he asked a question. Worst of all, he found he was checking the mirror after he'd spent time with her, as though the surgery had failed, as if Alton Lowenthal was showing through.

CHAPTER EIGHTEEN

Dave had avoided other Jews for years, but he welcomed Wolff as a visitor. He did everything he could to make the chaplain understand that. But he also knew perfectly well why the big man remained wary, why there was always caution in his eyes.

He couldn't expect anything different. Dave remembered perfectly well that he'd thrown a spit bowl at Wolff, and cursed him.

Dave would have liked to explain that at the time he'd thrown the spit basin his mind had been muddled. He hadn't been responding to Wolff Blumen, chaplain. In his confusion before his second surgery Wolff and Al Logan had been some part of the Nazi death camp where he'd believed he was being held. They'd been guard and fellow inmate. But Dave couldn't explain any of that with out bringing up all sorts of other things that he had no intention of sharing.

The day Robin left Wolff announced that there had been great excitement at their house when Shayna and Sunny discovered that they were "almost twins."

"Sunny's birthday is sometime soon, right?"

"Yes, it's the twentieth."

"Well, Shayna's birthday is the twenty-fifth, and apparently that qualifies as 'almost twins.' So they've decided that they're going to have a joint birthday party at our house, 'for kosher' as Sunny now says.

"It'll make it much easier on Robin. She mentioned that she didn't know how to manage a party for Sunny while you were here. Faiga and I want to make sure it was okay with you. There are already plans to bring you a piece of cake, with a candle.

"Faiga is happy to have the party if it will help Robin. They've become very good friends, those two, my wife and yours. Every morning it's a regular *Kaffeklatch*. I'm grateful. Sometimes Faiga gets very depressed living here. You can hardly blame her. Most of the people in our community are much older than we are. They're very kind, very good to us, but it's as though we are their children. Having Robin around has been so good for Faiga.

"She says Robin is one of the best listener she's ever run into; and very smart and sensible, too. So if you feel your ears burning one morning, don't be surprised. I'm sure that the minute I walk out the door, the subject is husbands."

When Wolff spoke about Robin so admiringly, a feeling Dave didn't like rippled through him. Jealously, as though he owned her. He was disgusted with himself.

He'd always appreciated Robin, but she was shy and cautious. Most people just never found out she was so smart and terrific. But now she had a fan club it seemed, and no one acknowledged that he had been the charter member.

Several of the aides on the floor were as enthusiastic about Robin as Wolff. Robin had run an aerobics class for the staff in the hospital gymnasium, as a 'Thank You' for Dave's care. Dave had thought it was a great idea. But at this moment it seemed to him that every male aide and orderly on the floor had fallen slightly in love with Robin.

Of course, Dave told himself, during his most realistic moments, it might just seem to him that every conversation led back to Robin because he felt guilty about keeping so many secrets from her. Even when she came back, after everything his accountant and the others would tell her, there would still be secrets.

If every man praising Robin made him jealous, implied criticism didn't make things any better

During one of their phone conversations, his accountant had suggested that perhaps Robin shouldn't be trusted with all the information Dave wanted to share.

"Why wouldn't I trust her? I trust her with my kid. I'd trust her with my life."

"Okay, okay, Dave, I hear you. But you've certainly never trusted her up to this point. I have to assume that your judgment when you're up and around is better than when you're in bed and dependant. I just don't want you to do anything now that you'll be sorry about later. Go slow."

"I don't want to go slow. I should have told her all this stuff years ago."

"Well, then, why didn't you?"

The main purpose of Jess' questions was professional, but Dave could also sense that his accountant didn't mind putting him on the spot. Jess had never met Robin. Also, he'd often pointed out that he had difficulty giving meaningful advices when big sections of Dave's life were secret.

Dave couldn't blame Jess for the advice he was giving, or for turning the knife just a little.

"You know, Dave, never mind trust. This is a lot to absorb in one meeting. Maybe she should stick around longer, so that we can go over things with her more slowly."

"No, I need...we, Sunny needs her back. Robin will want to get back too. It's Sunny's birthday soon."

"I know when her birthday is; that's not until the twentieth. There's plenty of time," Jess said.

"Just go over the will with her, and over all the insurance policies. Show her what the arrangements are if I predecease her. Let her know what she'll have to manage should anything happen to me."

If anyone had been in the room with Dave when he talked about Robin, they would have seen the torment in his eyes, the tension in his fist gripping the telephone.

"Just remember not to go into detail on the amounts I put in for my family. Tell her they're straight bequests, no names. Robin doesn't need to know who they are. She won't ask. It's all there, right?"

"Of course it's all there, Dave. But you're sure it's not a lack of trust, right? And, I'll say it again: it's a lot to absorb. It's taken you years to accumulate a sizable estate, and you want Robin to understand it in one two-hour meeting."

"She's a lot brighter than I am," Dave said dryly.

The accountant wasn't amused. "She'll have to be. I think I'm sorry we started all this. It would have been better for you to eat the expenses and fly one of us out there."

"No, this is the right way to do it. I want Robin to understand as much as possible, from you. You can give her the scope, and the way things are being done. You can explain my thinking. A list wouldn't do that. It's okay if you leave some questions unanswered, like the names, the relationships. I'm probably going to catch it from her anyway when she gets back here, because I never told her about all this before. But, I never really knew how…and…

"And?"

Dave could tell that his accountant in Minneapolis was just as curious about him as his doctor in Sioux Falls.

"Never mind…"

"Okay. Never mind. It's all as usual. But I've got one more question, and one more thing to say.

"The question is: do you want me to contact the rest of your family? They don't know about the accident yet.

"And, Dave, what I just said about Robin: I don't want to malign a lady I've never met. But, I have to point out to you that there are a lot of assets here. She has access to some of them, no questions asked. What if she decides not to come back? Are you sure your first instincts about her weren't right?"

"There were no instincts involved," Dave said. "And even if there were, they never had anything to do with not trusting her. Now, I have to figure out a way round the…some of the mess I've made. I never should have started this way, and then I shouldn't have kept on this way. But never mind, it's done."

Jess finally let him off the hook. "Done is done, as they say. We'll all be interested to meet the mystery man's mystery lady. It really is too bad you didn't do this a long time ago."

Why had he not told Robin a long time ago, Dave thought, not for the first time, as he hung up. But, told her what? Told her, along with everything else, that not until Sunny's birth had he'd realized that he'd given his own child the one thing he thought might keep her safe: a non-Jewish mother. How could he ever explain what that really meant to him?

Should he have told her that he had a small fortune, in case they ever had need of it? How would he tell her that now? How to explain that he'd never mentioned that fact before?

Dave knew that he'd made himself an unparalleled architect of secrets. He had created real, solid barriers to keep everyone, especially Robin and Sunny, absolutely safe. But he hadn't told anyone how to get inside his structure. And, he hadn't allowed for the fact that one day he might want to get out.

CHAPTER NINETEEN

olff had been keeping a close watch on his charges. He'd seen that Al made Robin nervous. He'd certainly realized that at first Al Logan spent far more time at the hospital than a normal news story would have required. Given what he knew about both Al and Dave, he needed to be in touch with them both. Visiting Dave was a simple matter. To talk to Al he only had to call KLON every day or two. After a couple of those calls, everyone at the station seemed to know him. The young woman who answered the phone that Monday morning obviously thought that clergy deserved special consideration. Although, as always, he had identified himself simply as 'Wolff Blumen,' she responded "Good Morning, Rabbi," and transferred him to the managing editor of the station.

"I'm sorry Al Logan isn't in, Rabbi. Is there something we can help you with? He said he's likely to be gone for a few days. I can get a message to him to call you. He left for Minneapolis."

"Minneapolis?" Even on casual consideration, it seemed an unlikely coincidence that Al Logan and Robin would have left for the same city on the same day. As far as Wolff knew, no one, including Robin, had mentioned that Al had a trip like that planned.

"Yes, he goes there, or at least he goes away, every few months. It's like that with this kind of talent, Rabbi. They like to keep in touch with their peers, to know what's out there. Logan's damn good, you know. He's really too good for a small market like this. It's likely he'll be leaving us soon, although don't tell him I said that. That's the kind of remark that could cost me money. This time he gave us shorter notice than usual. He's been very good about not going when we really need him. Don't tell him I said that, either. Shall I leave a message for him to call you?"

Wolff declined to leave a message.

He didn't say anything about Al's absence to Dave. He'd heard about Dave throwing the newsman out of his room. Wolff heard a great deal of gossip, because he always kept his ears open when he was near a nursing station or at other gathering spots in the hospital.

Before Robin left for Minneapolis, when Dave had first emerged from his coma, and was already operating 'like a tycoon' as one of the nurses said, there had been discussion about Al Logan

One of the nurses, a no-nonsense hospital veteran, sniffed with disdain at the mention of Al. "Good for Dave! I'd have thrown that news-hound out a long time ago. It always looked to me like he was just hunting for an excuse to hit on Robin. I don't think she'd know a bad guy if he came up to her and introduced himself as the big bad wolf."

"He's cute, though," another nurse said, giggling.

"Razkowski doesn't thinks he's so cute," said one of the interns. "I noticed that when Dave finally told Logan to get out, Robin looked plenty relieved."

Wolff and Dave never mentioned Al Logan's name in their conversation. However, Robin's name kept coming up.

"She's gone to do my bidding, as any good woman should," Dave told Wolff, obviously trying to keep things light.

"What about her own bidding? That comes up at my house every so often."

"Well, Rabbi, when Robin finds out all the information I've sent her to collect and she realizes what I've sort of neglected to tell her over time, I'm probably have to do her bidding for years, just to make it up to her."

"That doesn't seem to worry you much, from what I can see."

"Don't kid yourself. If I wasn't lying here, essentially unable to defend myself, I'd be worried that she'd come back and deck me. But Robin...well...she doesn't get mad."

"Maybe there's never been any justification before," the bearded man said, wanting to see Dave's reaction.

"I've thought about that, Rabbi, believe me. If you're right, you may have to rescue me again. We'll have to wait until she gets back to find out what happens."

"Maybe one of your angels will come back to save you," Wolff said. Dave had told him about his vision of the rescue workers.

"I don't know that they make return engagements," Dave said.

✡

The first time Dave thought he saw angels he was four years old.

He had been sitting with his mother, in the second floor women's section of the tiny traditional synagogue his parents had joined as soon as they immigrated to Detroit. His mother, Margarita, had wrapped her arm tight around his waist and had lifted him so that he could see down over the solid half wall to the main floor where his father prayed with the other men. Below him stretched a sea of prayer-shawled figures. As he'd looked down, all the men lifted their prayer shawls up over their heads to make their own personal space for their private prayers. The shawls, white with dark blue or black stripes at the ends and with knotted fringes at each corner, billowed like wings.

"Look, Mommy," he'd said, in the carrying, bell-clear voice of an excited child, "There are angels down there!"

His mother always remembered that moment. "People all over the *shul* heard you. I felt mortified. They would say that my child didn't know how to behave in synagogue. But it made you a pet. They still talk about the 'angels.' Even though we only came for *Yizkor*, they would let you go anywhere."

Margarita Razkowski's memories were far more benevolent than those of her youngest child. Dave barely remembered those angels. What he remembered too clearly was the man his father became when they were in the synagogue.

Dave only attended synagogue a few times a year throughout his childhood, and then only for tearful, emotional, memorial services. He'd never been in a synagogue on a joyous holiday, or for anything celebratory like a wedding or a baby naming.

Jacob Razkowski had not been a religious man before the war. He did not become one after. He raised his children as he had been raised, as secular Socialist Jews. To Jacob, Judaism was political. Being a Jew involved history and culture, the Yiddish language and literature. Religious duties were only included if people choose to perform them. There was certainly no requirement for belief.

As an adolescent in Poland, Jacob's most important milieu had been the youth movement of the politically radical Labor Zionists. In fact, in later years he would joke that if Hitler hadn't hated him because he was a Jew, he would have locked him up anyway, as a trade unionist.

But, religious or not, Jacob Razkowski's first act on arriving in the United States had been to declare that the week they came to the U.S.A. would be the *yarzheit,* the yearly memorial, for all the members of their families and for all his comrades who had died.

They didn't know the actual dates when individual Holocaust victims had perished. So, to Jacob, the day he finished with Europe, the day he brought his family to a new country, seemed the ideal time for a memorial.

The Razkowskis, Jacob, Margarita and their oldest son, landed in New York in early September, 1952. A few days later, on the Sunday before Labor Day, they were greeted by Hebrew Immigrant Aid Society workers at the train station in Detroit where they were to settle. When the people from HIAS asked Jacob Razkowski what he wanted to do first, he said, "I have to say *Kaddish.*"

They were escorted to *Beit T'fillah,* House of Prayer, a synagogue founded by Holocaust survivors who had arrived before them. Their hosts waited respectfully while

Jacob sat through the morning service so he could recite the traditional memorial prayer, *Kaddish*.

Thereafter, despite Jacob's anti-religious ways and the a-religious environment in their home, *Beit T'fillah* was the Razkowski family synagogue. Every year, even at the beginning when the family had almost no money, Jacob paid his annual dues.

Also, during the entire first week of September, Jacob and his whole family attended regular early morning and evening services as mourners. It was Dave's only exposure to synagogue Judaism. He knew nothing about Conservative or Reform Jewish practices, because all his friends were children of the survivor community.

Jacob Razkowski lit memorial candles during his week of mourning. Every night at sundown he lined up the candles for a group of his dead on the kitchen counter. The candles in their clear glass holders stood on a sheet of burnished metal to protect the house from fire. The metal sheet might have protected the house, but nothing protected Dave. Each candle burned for at least twenty-four hours. And each year, as they received confirmation of more deaths through the Red Cross, more candles were added.

By the time Dave was in grade school they had accumulated the names of more than one hundred family members and friends known to have die.

The Razkowski family's week of official remembrance became a conflagration. One day's candles would still be burning when the next day's candles were ignited. Each candle stood in its separate clear glass container. Dave knew exactly who each candle had been lit for: which candle was for the man who had fought with the Resistance, which two were for his mother's parents who were believed to have starved to death. Most of the candles flamed for those who had been gassed and burned in the concentration camps that Jacob and Margarita had miraculously survived.

Every year, during that week, at home and in the synagogue, Dave saw his father turn into a different man.

Ordinarily Jacob Razkowski was a cheerful person, a businessman and a calm assured craftsman. He took an active part in his community and also took an interest in all of his children's activities. By the time Dave was born he was even a reasonably prosperous man.

Jacob's first job, arranged by HIAS, had been in a furniture factory. After ten years in that factory he had been able to open his own plant, where he made handsome outdoor furniture.

But, during his memorial week, the calm, prosperous, confident, Jacob Razkowski disappeared. It seemed to Dave that his father actually became smaller, thinner, and that his face became drawn and grey. It was as though his father was agonizingly hungry that whole week, but couldn't eat. As Jacob set the house alight with his candles, Dave would have given anything to be able to comfort him, or to take on his pain. How he wished his father would work to forget instead of to remember.

But Jacob's rituals were to preserve memories. Each year he again explained exactly what he was doing to his children.

"It shouldn't be *Kaddish* that I say, because it is a prayer that honors God, a prayer of acceptance. For me, I don't honor God, nor do I believe He cares, if He exists at all. I do not accept what happened. But my beliefs are not important here. My family, my parents, all of them, they would expect a *Kaddish* from me. Them I honor, in a way they would have expected and understood. For my comrades, perhaps it should be something else, but we never talked about it. By the time we realized what was happening, to talk about *Kaddish* would have seemed like inviting death. We were too afraid. So for them, too, our traditional ways will have to serve. The important thing is to remember them and what happened to them. That is the part of our tradition that I can honor; the need to remember."

Dave didn't believe that his father had ever been afraid, not even of death. It seemed to him that with candles and prayers his father invited death into their home every year. If the job of remembering required such bravery, Dave couldn't imagine even attempting it on his own. His father had to be a hero, just to take on such a job. Each time he heard his father's explanations, Dave knew he would never measure up.

Jacob seemed to take it for granted that eventually his children would do as he did. He had presented his sons with their own prayer shawls when they were thirteen. The family referred to that ceremony as a *bar mitzvah,* and since Dave didn't know anything different, it sufficed. Dave rarely wore his prayer shawl. It wasn't like his father's. The coloring was the same, black and white, but it was nowhere near the size of the all-enveloping garment his father wore.

"It's more modern, and more your size," his father said about the prayer shawl he had selected for Dave. But Dave knew that the smaller prayer shawl had been made for people like him and his brother, who would never have an opportunity to show how brave and strong they were. A real *tallit* like his father's had to be earned by facing death.

Even after his thirteenth birthday, when Dave always sat with the men, he chose to plant himself beside his father, sharing one wing of his father's large *tallit*. His brother, so much older, did exactly the same, sitting on the other side. Without discussion the two had made themselves into an honor guard and protection for their father. It seemed to them that Jacob Razkowski needed both. They never questioned that their father could be both strong and frail at the same time.

Jacob's prayer shawl was large enough for the three of them. It was made of off-white wool and it covered him to the ankles when he draped it over his shoulders. Every man in the synagogue wore an almost identical shawl. No one had ever explained what the prayer shawl or any other synagogue symbol meant to Dave. Sitting there beside his father, he worked out his own ideas. He had decided that the dark stripes on the end of the prayer shawls were in memory of the black and white striped uniforms concentration camp victims had worn.

Dave was in college before he had any other experience of Judaism.

The year he began college, he felt compelled to do something during the Jewish High Holidays. His father would be in their synagogue in Detroit for *Yizkor*, and he was determined to support him by attending in Ann Arbor. Services were being held in a bright, cheerful multi-purpose room at Hillel. He'd called to find out what time *Yizkor* would be held but services was running a little behind schedule. In this liberal service, men and women sat together, and many of the prayers were in English.

As he waited for the memorial service he paged through the prayer book. To his relief he immediately found the traditional *Kaddish*, with an English translation provided. As his father had said, the prayer spoke of glorifying God. But he was surprised to find that it didn't contain anything else. How could his father say only these words? If you used words you didn't believe, what was the value of what you said?

Worse than the words of the prayer being made clear to him, were the people all around him. Very few people had come only for *Yizkor*. Most had been there all morning. Despite the fact that the holiday was somewhat somber; Dave found himself surrounded by light-hearted young men and women. To him, they were only going through the motions of mourning.

He saw almost no proper prayer shawls, somber black and white. Most of the shawls there were in brilliant colors. Some had fanciful designs: Israeli landscapes, imagined Biblical scenes, a rainbow. None were all-enveloping garments of hard-surfaced wool. Most were made of silk that glowed like the colors in a stained glass window.

The prayer shawl, a garment that spoke only of sorrow and memory to Dave, almost as though it was a shroud, was a gorgeously colored silken adornment to these people.

The feeling in this temporary High Holy Day synagogue was also wrong. Some of the participants were clearly dealing with personal loses, but there was nothing like the intensity of sorrow that was obvious in his father's synagogue. Dave didn't stop to ask himself how anything but the Holocaust could generate such overwhelming grief.

Dave knew what his father was enduring at that moment at *Beit T'fillah*. He would never be able to mourn like that, be fit to belong to that synagogue. You had to be a hero to pray there. Every man and woman there had done the things his parents had done. They had survived Nazi labor camps or death camps. They had seen their families die, along with most of their friends. And several times each year all of them came to synagogue voluntarily and confronted death again.

Dave had taken off his prayer shawl and skullcap, and left the campus Hillel building.

It was his first attempt to duplicate his father's ritual of suffering. But it wasn't possible. Nor was it possible to talk to his father about it. He was left with the uncomfortable feeling that he would have to find his own way to mourn. What that might be Dave couldn't imagine. He couldn't think of any way he might one day lift the burden of grief from his father's shoulders either.

CHAPTER TWENTY

hen Robin arrived in Minneapolis the house looked strange to her, as though someone else might live there.

She had never before driven such a long distance alone. Just stopping felt like a reward. She sat in the Wrangler for a few minutes, grateful for the stillness.

Finally she hoisted her duffel bag and got out of the car, leaving the Jeep in the driveway. She was too tired to drive it around to the garage at the back of the house. She trudged up the five outside stairs and across the old-fashioned wooden porch that she and Dave had restored. The porch's screen door slapped shut behind her. The big front door of the house stuck a moment longer than usual, as though it resented being left alone. Robin pulled the deadbolt key back slightly, toward herself, and turned her wrist with authority. They had refinished the original old door. It was oak, with a heavy oval of beveled glass set in, surrounded by wooden trim carved in a heavy braid. It needed just the right amount of hip put into it to open, and that had to be just as the key was inserted and the knob turned. It finally yielded to Robin's careful choreography.

Once inside, she placed her bag on the floor and walked along the long side hall from the front to the back of the house. She passed by the living room, the family room where they had packed for Dave's trip, then the dining room. As she'd passed each room she reached in and flipped on the lights. She needed the company.

After a few minutes she went to inspect the upstairs. Everything was as she had left it. She frowned at a partially opened drawer and folded mirrored doors left askew in the master bedroom, as though she ought to deduct points from the passing grade she'd hoped to earn. She pushed the drawer shut and partially closed the mirrored doors, making sure they didn't directly align with the bed. She didn't want to think about what they had reflected before.

Robin missed her sex life with Dave terribly, but she didn't willing think about it. She had never been able to say very much about their love making to Dave.

The rooms were dusty but otherwise just the same. In Sunny's room Dave had installed bunks behind a huge cut out of a castle painted an improbable pink and purple, Sunny's favorite colors. Anyone who saw Sunny's room oohed and aahed over the bed. Dave had created a ladder 'stairway' to the top bunk, and castle 'windows' in front of each bed.

The 'castle' included two deep wide drawers for toys under the bottom bunk. The rest of the storage in the small room, including a little desk for when Sunny started grade school, had been built into the wall opposite the bunk bed, with shuttered bi-fold doors and sliders to cover the whole expanse.

This was the way little girls should be raised, Robin told herself. The way she had grown up had been all wrong. No child should be dragged around following the men her mother wanted to 'snag.' Never, in all those years, had she had a room of her own. At first she'd shared a room with her brother. Later she'd shared her mother's room when there was no man around.

Robin shuddered a little at the memory of her childhood. She wanted stability and beauty around Sunny. They'd had that all the years she'd been with Dave. Maybe it wasn't total, married stability, but it was probably as close as most people ever got. It was too precious to lose.

She frowned at the idea that it could be at risk. She knew that something had changed between her and Dave, something she couldn't yet name and didn't want to face.

She surveyed Sunny's room again. She'd made the pink and purple jester-style topper for the window herself. It had been the first time she'd ever tried any kind of craft project. She'd even figured out how to decorate her creation with gold metal studs on each pointed felt piece.

Dave's efforts and her own had made a dream of a room for a little girl. A little girl needed parents who could provide things like a safe, pretty room.

Sunny would continue to have that, Robin assured herself. And she would be, she already was, a strong, independent-minded little girl. That could only come from self-confidence. She knew she didn't have enough of that herself, but she was determined that Sunny would.

Sunny displayed impressive strength of mind already. Like the first day Robin had brought her to visit Dave at the hospital. Robin and Faiga had agreed that Sunny needed to see her father, even though Dave remained in a coma. Robin had consulted the doctors, and she and Faiga had agreed that they would tell Sunny that her Daddy was fast asleep, a special kind of sleep that helped people who were hurt. Sunny had been as well prepared as possible.

In the Wrangler, driving to the hospital, Robin had explained over and over, that Daddy might be asleep for many days, but then he would wake up and, once all his 'ouchies' had healed, he would be fine. It might take a long time, Robin cautioned her daughter. It might even take until she was six, two whole birthdays away.

At the hospital, Sunny had walked up to Dave's bed and looked at him somberly. She'd reached out one finger and traced an invisible line along the pillar of the white cast that reached to the middle of Dave's chest. She'd even tapped Dave's arm very gently, almost the way a housewife might prod a chicken or a piece of fish she was considering for a meal.

"Faiga and Shayna say special prayers for people who are hurt or sick," Sunny said, looking at Robin and ignoring Dave.

"That's really good," Robin had said fervently. "Do you think they would say one for Daddy?"

"I suppose," the little girl said. "But I think they should say one for this man." She pointed at Dave as though she had never seen him before in her life.

"Baby, this is Daddy!" Robin hadn't known whether to laugh or cry at the expression on her daughter's face. Clearly this unresponsive, supine figure was not an acceptable Daddy.

Sunny had been willing to reconsider, though. She'd stood on tiptoe and looked at Dave's face again, then walked the length of the bed, around the end and up the other side, her finger again tracing an invisible line. Robin followed her. Once on the other side of the bed the little girl had peered at Dave's face from her new perspective. True, what she'd seen hadn't been very reassuring. Dave looked awful, even to Robin, who knew that the scrapes and bruises on his face were the least of his problems.

"It's a very high bed," Robin had said to her daughter. "Would you like me to lift you up so you can see him better?"

"Sure," Sunny had said, and she'd raised her arms to be lifted by Robin from behind.

Hanging in Robin's grasp, Sunny examined Dave's face one more time. She even put out one tentative finger, just barely touching his face,

"That's not my daddy," Sunny had announced with calm authority once Robin put her down. "My Daddy is on the top of a BIG mountain."

Standing in the doorway of Sunny's room, Robin would have liked to borrow some of her daughter's strength of mind to face the tasks ahead. Sunny's approach at finding an injured Daddy closely resembled the kind of thing Dave might have done. If Dave wanted something to be, it was; and if he didn't, then it didn't exist. Not a bad way, although hard on those who had to deal with the rejected reality.

Consistency wasn't a problem with this kind of world view. Only three days after Sunny has been so dismissive of the comatose, injured Dave, she was equally enthusiastic once he was awake.

"Daddy," Sunny had shrieked joyously. Then she'd clambered up on the bed to hug and kiss him, to show him her crafts, to draw pictures on his cast. Sunny had never again referred to the other man, the one she thought Faiga and Shayna should pray for.

But she couldn't just stand there in the doorway of her daughter's room. Her ruminations were just an excuse to put off the work she had to do. Too bad Sunny's technique of making reality bend didn't work for her; she couldn't pretend with her daughter's fervor.

Then the shrill of the doorbell frightened Robin out of her reverie. They never had company, and nobody knew she was in the city. She pulled herself away from the doorway and headed downstairs. Amazingly, her visitor was her neighbor, Tovah Feldner. Even more surprising, the young rabbi didn't have her usual neighborly smile. Tonight she looked stern.

Robin found herself fumbling with the knob, wondering what she would say to Tovah. When the door was opened Tovah said, in a voice that implied authority, "I just saw your lights. Where have you been?"

At the sound of her question she frowned, which made her mobile face look younger. She must have recognized her tone of voice, because she continued in a much more measured way. "I'm sorry. I shouldn't attack like that. But we've really been worried. Dan knew that Dave was leaving on a trip. But then you disappeared too, except your car didn't."

Tovah pointed in the general direction of the garage where Robin had left the little Toyota that she drove to work and to do errands.

Tovah continued, "It's been days and days, and we had no idea where you might have gone. Is everything all right?"

Robin realized that she was standing there in the doorway, forgetting her manners, not asking Tovah to come in. Despite her quizzing Tovah seemed less intimidating than usual. Tovah was shorter than she'd thought, which helped somehow. And tonight the rabbi wasn't dressed in one of her formal suits. She wore a sweatshirt and jeans, and all her dark curly hair tumbled around her face. Robin hoped she'd left the kitchen tidy enough for company.

When she noticed Robin's frown Tovah was direct, quick to provide a reason not to prolong their encounter. "Do you want me to go, Robin?" She even looked a little unsure of herself, the way Robin often felt. Robin had never imagined making anyone feel like that.

"Oh, no, I'm sorry. Come in. It's just that I never thought to tell anyone. I never thought you'd worry. I didn't imagine you ever knew where I was, whether we were around or not."

"Well, you've always been right here, next door. There wasn't anything to worry about until now." Tovah tried to joke, to lighten the intense mood that had suddenly come over the two women. "Dave mentioned to Dan that he was going rock climbing. That it's an annual trip. But he said, really specifically, that you weren't going. But then you and Sunny just disappeared. We didn't know what to think."

Tovah had followed Robin down the hall and into the perfectly tidy kitchen by then. They stood there, neither one of them knowing what to do next. Robin had often wondered how she might go about making friends with Tovah. She could never imagine that they had anything in common. Apparently, Tovah took being neighbors as some sort of a commitment. Or perhaps Dave and Dan were better friends than Dave had indicated. Dave did seem to know more about Leah Goldin's physical problems than Robin had ever guessed.

"Did you drive in? Where are Dave and Sunny? Is everyone okay?" Tovah asked her questions so rapid-fire that Robin couldn't do much more than blink at each one.

"Yes," she said, answering the first question, and then "No," for the last question. "Dave's had an accident, but he's okay. Well, that is, he'll be okay, but it might take a while. He'll need lots of physical therapy. I came back to get some papers for him, business, power of attorney, you know, and I..." She paused, unsure of how much she needed to tell.

Tovah took a deep breath. She looked sympathetic and unhappy all at the same time. "I'm sorry. Sorry about the accident. Sorry, I was going way too fast. I tend to do that. You have to stop me when I do it. Really, now that we know you're safe, I can just go home, leave you alone if that's what you need right now, though I'd rather not."

Robin blinked at such candor. But Faiga Blumen was a little like that too, so fortunately she'd had some recent practice in dealing with people who were so direct. "Oh, please, can you stay? I'd love some company. Coffee? Would you like a cup of coffee, or tea? Please, sit down."

"I'll tell you what," Tovah said, speaking more slowly. Robin realized Tovah was watching her response closely. "I'm going to get some muffins or bagels out of the freezer–my mother left me a batch of stuff–and then I'm going to come right back here for that cup of coffee. Dan will mind the kids and get them to bed. He's better at that than I am, anyway."

Robin had to work to keep her face neutral. She'd never heard a woman casually admit to a thing like that.

Tovah didn't seem to be aware of having said anything unusual. She continued on, making plans for both of them. For a moment she sounded like a waitress.

"Bagels or Muffins?" Then, decisive again, she answered her own question. "Muffins, I think. And, I'll bring some milk. Do you have coffee?"

Robin pointed to the coffee maker. "The coffee is in the freezer."

"Good. I'll be back. Just give me a few minutes. Then you can tell me the whole story."

Despite Tovah's somewhat high-handed style, she proved to be an excellent listener. Her face mirrored her sympathy. She didn't interrupt. Once she reached out and patted Robin's hand in a motherly way.

People get to be friends like this, Robin thought, as she recounted what had happened in the previous weeks.

"Poor thing," Tovah said when she told her about Sunny's original reaction to the chaplain. And there was a flash of something almost hostile when Robin said, "I guess he's more a regular rabbi. He has– you know–he wears those dark clothes."

Robin even described Wolff and Faiga Blumen's household. Tovah didn't interrupt that either, although she laughed when Robin mentioned Faiga's kosher chocolate-chip peanut-butter cookies.

"We can talk about that sometime if you want to," Tovah said. "God, you've had quite a time. Will Dave really be okay? You don't need emergency funds or anything?"

"Well, I thought we did, that I'd need to work in Sioux Falls, but Dave had already arranged for disability insurance. I didn't even know…" She stopped. It sounded irresponsible not to know, and she didn't want to get into the subject of their marital status.

"Well, I have disability, too, but Dan doesn't, of course. Dave would want protection, since he's self-employed, I mean. And, of course, you wouldn't have thought to take the policies with you when you went flying off in an emergency like that."

"I have to go and gather up the stuff he needs. I have a list." Robin glanced up stairs. "His office is on the third floor. I almost never go up there."

"Would you like some company, or will it distract you? I don't want to intrude."

"No, please. Company would be great." Ordinarily Robin wouldn't have thought of letting someone upstairs, into Dave's private office. But for once what she needed seemed more important. "I'd love some company," she repeated, as much to convince herself as to invite Tovah. "You could talk to me. I need to get about a dozen files. I have the keys." She pulled them out of her pocket, as though they proved that she had authority.

Tovah said, "Maybe you can give me a tour while we go upstairs. Everyone on the block loves what you did with the house. It was marvelous to watch you and Dave turn it around. It's so attractive. Dan would love to do more with ours, but we're still renting, so we have to wait."

Tovah was a great audience, admiring the double-sided fireplace between the family room and the living room. When the two women went upstairs she was enthusiastic about Sunny's room.

"Leah would love this room. Ari would love the ladder," she said.

As they mounted the short, flight of stairs to the partial third floor Tovah commented, "Dave has a nice set-up, being able to work at home like this."

Dave had stained the new oak floor he'd installed on the third floor golden brown. The color looked especially rich and dark tonight. The square newel post at the very top of the stairway had an old fashioned, frosted light fixture set into the top. It was shaped like a fat flame. Dave had rewired it and put in a small bulb. It glowed as they came up the stairs, adding warmth to the paneling in the small, square hall and casting some of its light into Dave's tidy, low-ceilinged office when Robin unlocked the door.

Robin gestured to Tovah to take Dave's big desk chair. Tovah angled the chair back from the desk, placing it in front of an unusually deep, built-in bookcase. She glanced at the titles.

"Design books and nature stuff, hmmm? I always want to know what people read," she said.

Robin, concentrating on opening Dave's files, just nodded. Dave's security system looked like it might be complicated, but she managed it without any trouble. He had added metal flaps that clamped over the drawers and locked. Who was he protecting his records from?

As Robin started through the files, she noticed several she would have liked to examine. None of them were on her list.

"Illinois" said one file. Dave had lived there at one time. It was close to the "Insurance" file, one she had pulled out. Another file, fat and bulging with yellowing papers, said "Razkowski, J." She passed it on the way to "Razkowski, WILL," one of the files on Dave's list. The will file held only a few sheets of paper. Razkowski, J. had to be a relative. Why did Dave have so much material on him or her?

FELDEFING was written in bold letters on one file. Was that a place? It didn't sound like the name of a person. But she didn't have the nerve to handle any of the files not on the list. After all, Dave was entitled to privacy from a neighbor he hardly knew. But was he entitled to total privacy from her? She told herself that Dave wouldn't want her to look at his private papers. But, it was getting much more difficult to honor some of the things Dave wanted.

A new voice inside Robin had been clamoring for attention for days. Being at home made it even louder. Why isn't it your business, it demanded? All this certainly impacts on your life and on the life of your child. Why are all these things so private?

Behind her, Tovah kept up a relaxed chatter somehow in tune with her own inner voice, as though Tovah wanted to help her along. Tovah never questioned Robin's right to be in this room, doing this job. Her attitude was validation.

"Almost done?" Tovah asked. "Toss me the list if you'd like. I'll read it off to you and you can check to make sure you've got them all."

Dave's computer monitor glowed in the light. It wasn't on, but the screen looked out at her as though it was a great eye of the house. Robin knew very little about computers. This one seemed to be a surrogate for Dave.

She handed Tovah the list and, responding to Tovah's gesture for something to write with, reached across Dave's desk to pull a fat marking pen from a mug full of pens. Without noting Tovah's exact position, she handed it back toward her with one extended arm.

Tovah tilted forward in Dave's big chair to take the pen, but the chair snapped level more quickly than she'd expected. In the act of bracing her feet on the floor Tovah missed the pen. It dropped from Robin's hand, rolling right past Tovah, then disappearing under the bookcase. That was a surprise, because the bookcase appeared to be built in very snugly, right down to the floor.

There were fleeting seconds of silence. Then, Tovah and Robin looked at each other, surprised. The sound was unmistakable: plink...plink...plink, the beat of a pen bouncing down a flight of stairs. It went on and on, fainter and fainter, continuing on a long way. Then, the office took on a new, uneasy silence, charged with the unexpressed questions of both women.

Neither of them commented, but simultaneously both women squatted down and each stuck a hand beneath the strip of molding that looked like it touched the floor. It was a deliberate illusion. A hand-span beyond the front edge of the bookcase the floor stopped abruptly. There was only empty space.

The women stood. Robin couldn't think of anything to say. Tovah obviously didn't want to comment.

"Dave covered up the old servant's staircase," she finally suggested.

"There never was one," Robin said emphatically. Her mind raced. This wasn't her imagination. This wasn't middle of the night weird ideas about what Dave might or might not be doing squirreled away in his upstairs office. These were some of the questions Robin had asked herself from time to time, but never fully acknowledged.

What was going on in her own house? How can there be a whole set of stairs back there, stair that didn't exist when we bought the house?

Everything that had happened in the last weeks had made Robin braver. Tovah's unexpected presence helped.

If choosing sides or keeping secrets became necessary, Robin thought she could count on her.

"I don't know what all this is about."

Tovah's nod seemed to say, "I can see that."

There was nothing left to say. Instead, Robin poked around in the bookcase shelves and then, hooking her fingers under a strip of molding that finished off the front vertical edge, she pulled.

The whole bookcase swung forward. There was the momentary illusion that it was falling over. Robin jumped back, gesturing for Tovah to do the same. But the bookcase wasn't falling. It opened as smoothly as any door, on silent hinges hidden in the back.

"A secret annex," Tovah said, her voice so subdued Robin barely caught the words.

The two of them were standing above a substantial set of stairs that began at the level of the office floor and angled quite sharply down into the interior of the house.

The stairs were new construction. Robin recognized the light fixture at the top of the staircase. It was just like the fixtures Dave had installed in all the closets. He'd selected them because they ran on batteries and could be put in without extra wiring. Tap the face of the light and it went on. In two minutes or so, it went off. If you tapped it twice, it stayed on until you tapped it off. Robin reached down and touched it with tentative fingers. It responded, flooding the new, clean, white wood stairway with a cold bluish glow.

The stairs were neatly made, Dave's work. The walls around them weren't finished in any normal way. Rather, every square inch of wall space around the stairs had been converted into shelves. They were stocked, several items deep, between the studs. Food and other house-hold supplies had been neatly stored away.

Robin shook her head in disbelief. It must have taken Dave months to buy all this stuff. How could she not have noticed it all coming into the house? Then she realized: Dave had done this during the times he'd come to Minneapolis alone, to work with the subcontractors. He'd had plenty of opportunity. The realization was like cold water in her face. Whatever this structure was, it had to have been in Dave's plans from the beginning. He must have thought about this for a very long time.

Looking down into the illuminated area though the narrow opening in the floor, Robin could see that the stairway ran from Dave's office to behind their bedroom. She couldn't believe it. Right behind the closet and the storage system Dave had built into the master bedroom, a secret stairway lined with food and other supplies.

Did Dave go back here and watch her in the bed-room when she thought she was alone? Could he see out from this space of his? Did he have other people back there watching them? That was crazy! Dave wasn't that kind of person.

The staircase looked like something a survivalist might build. Did Dave think the end of the world was coming? Did he believe someone might try to overthrow the government? There were people in lots of places, small towns in the Dakotas were she'd lived before, who did believe things like that; people who refused to pay their taxes for all sorts of weird reasons. She vaguely remembered Dave commenting on one such group in Fargo. There had been several incidents the last year they'd lived there, hate mailings and tombstones toppled in a graveyard. She remembered that the group involved was very clear that they hated blacks and Jews. Dave had laughed at them, said they were 'loonies.' Was his derision a cover for secretly agreeing with them? Did Dave think his family needed these kinds of emergency supplies? If he believed that, why would he keep it a secret from her?

Tovah was standing alongside her, waiting, watching closely, almost as though she could read the thoughts that ran through Robin's mind.

The expression on Tovah's face made it clear that she would not take the initiative in this case.

So, Robin was clearly the one in charge. And clearly, they had to explore. Having Tovah alongside supplied just the extra support she needed.

At a gesture from Robin, Tovah pulled the bookcase back as far as possible and set the heavy desk chair in front of it, making sure the rollers on the chair were locked fast. Neither of them wanted the door to shut. They could see heavy bolt latches on the bottom of the bookcase door, so that it could be locked from the inside. Clearly anyone behind the bookcase could keep their existence a secret from people in the house.

Robin tapped the light twice to keep it on, and then, stepping carefully, headed down the stairs. Tovah followed. The entrance was somewhat narrow and awkward, but once they were a little way in they found that Dave had built an especially sturdy banister. It functioned as a handhold and it kept the contents of many of the shelves neatly locked into place. Those shelves not directly protected by the banister, were secured with thin bungee cords. The selection included: dry soup mix, beans, and containers full of what looked like sugar, flour and pancake mix. Bottled water, cans of juice, dry milk powder passed under Robin's hand as they went slowly down the stairs. They passed one landing, stopped at the second. Now they would be level with the bedroom floor.

The landing was almost like a little room, wide and deep. Space beyond the size of the stairs had been cantilevered out, expanding each landing. No wonder the bedrooms in the house were smaller than she'd expected they would be. This was where the extra space had gone. On each landing there was a shelf set into the wall opposite the handrail. The shelf held a plastic bag with a label that said, "Bedding."

"He certainly thought of everything," Tovah said, and Robin nodded. It was like Dave to think of every detail on any project he undertook. But, in this case, she couldn't even begin to imagine what 'everything' might include.

Robin was still in shock, but she could see that Tovah was checking out the details of the stairway. At one point Tovah reached out experimentally and tried to lift a stair tread. "Extra space," she said to Robin. Her fingers searched a moment, as though they were seeking an understanding of the man who'd created the structure.

"Aha," she said and unsnapped something. She lifted the tread. "See? It's more storage."

They tried the other stairs in the immediate area. They were all hollow boxes, sturdily-built. Each was neatly finished, with a rough-textured safety strip along the front edge that gleamed in the dim light, little grains of sand like diamonds.

"Look at this," Tovah had found another cache. "First aid, a pharmacy almost. There's paper and pens, audio tapes, a camera, more first aid supplies, batteries, bottled water."

Every step held essential items, although the fact that they were hollow certainly wasn't obvious. Dave had lined them so that they didn't echo.

The tap-on, tap-off lights had been installed throughout. In addition, portable security lights that plugged into the house electrical system were in place.

"These landings are certainly big enough to sleep on." Robin barely heard Tovah's words. She was trying to understand what Dave had done here, and why. "This one would be tight for a man, but someone my size, or a child, certainly, would fit. There's probably a bigger one farther down the stairs, on the first floor."

Between the second and first floors of the house there was more food, but there were also books. Robin saw *Mein Kampf* and *The War Against the Jews*. A little green and white book that looked cheaply printed had a hand-lettered title: *Feldefing*. She had just seen that word on one of Dave's files.

Once they noticed the books the two of them stopped, balanced on the stairs, craning their necks to read the titles. The books started near the top of the staircase, they now realized, and were shelved in spots where only a tall person, like Dave, could easily reach them.

Tovah stretched up to her full five feet four inches, reached way up over her head and pulled three books at random from a shelf. Robin was reading titles, a shocked note in her voice.

"*The Holocaust in Europe, 1933-1945. An Atlas of World War II. Night,* by Eli Wiesel." Robin knew that name. Then, suddenly it was too much for her. She'd always had questions about Dave, but this had never occurred to her. She sat down on the stairs.

"Oh, my God," she wailed. "Dave is a Nazi; one of those awful people. I can't believe it."

"Don't believe it. Not yet," Tovah said. She looked serious, but determined. "Don't jump to any conclusions about him." She pulled at Robin's arm to get her up. Now Tovah took the lead, tapping the lights on as they came to a third landing and then finally a fourth, the largest one yet. It had a built-in writing surface angled out from the wall. On another wall there was a small sink with foot pedal controls. It was obviously connected to the house plumbing because it splashed water silently when Robin worked the 'Hot' tap.

"We're right behind the laundry room," she said. "This stairway has a slight curve in it. We're near the bathroom on the main floor. This is why Dave designed the house the way he did, with the laundry room on the first floor and the mud-room and a bathroom near the back door, next to the kitchen." Her face crumpled with hurt at the realization that none of it had been done for her convenience.

Robin leaned up against the wall for a moment, then jumped away when it moved behind her. Instead of a wall, she had leaned against a folding door that opened to reveal a whole bathroom, tiny but complete. Dave had even installed a shower.

There were other shocks in this part of the stairway-bunker. When they picked up the stair treads here they found "an arsenal," Tovah said, keeping her voice carefully neutral.

Robin couldn't imagine what her neighbor was thinking. Why on earth did Dave have all these guns and ammunition? What was he planning? Why was he so afraid?

Before this, Robin would have said that Dave wasn't afraid of anything. But this place had to be the result of fear, some kind of paranoia. The guns and bullets indicated that.

You couldn't call it anything less than an arsenal. Packed away in the stairs were several side arms and a rifle, all broken down. Alongside the guns, Dave had stacked innumerable boxes of ammunition in locked cases, securing it all under some kind of intricate webbing.

"He's certainly careful," Tovah said with something like admiration in her voice. She took Robin's arm, a gesture that seemed protective. "We haven't much farther to go."

"We'd better see it all," Robin agreed. They walked half a flight more, to what had been obvious almost from the top of the structure. The stairs stopped abruptly.

Suddenly, as though in a panic, Robin began to pound on the construction. "It can't stop here! There has to be another way in, and a way out!"

Then she realized that there was a trap-door mechanism set partially into the wall and partially into the floor of the area in front of them. She just had to lift the control bar toward herself. The whole apparatus was somewhat disguised by the pattern of the lumber, but quite obvious once you knew it was there. Robin heaved once, then again. The trapdoor pulled up and stayed up. A powerful spring held it in place. There were latches to lock it in place too, but they didn't seem necessary.

The two women knelt and looked through the trap door.

They were hovering a short distance above the basement floor. The structure was low enough that the trap could be reached and closed from below. Dave had ended his stairway in the basement, in a corner behind the furnace. There was very little headroom.

Large boulders of the original foundation made up the surrounding walls. It you didn't know the stairwell existed, it would be hard to find the entrance, even if you searched the basement.

A ladder had been hung on the wall a short distance away. To the innocent eye it would appear merely stored there. To Robin and Tovah it indicated how easily people could climb into the stairwell 'apartment' from the basement if they couldn't just swing themselves up.

It would be easy enough to draw the short ladder up through the trap and stash it in the stairwell on the inside. Then there would be no sign that there were people living above your head as long as they were quiet.

Tovah pointed to a flat panel set into the exterior wall of the house. Robin, who rarely needed to venture into the basement of her home, had noticed the panel once before, but never had a chance to examine it. Tovah followed her, moving cautiously. Dave had installed a new concrete floor in the basement before he'd started work on the house. It was medium gray and heavily textured. They wouldn't leave any incriminating dusty footprints behind.

"This is a very old house, like my parents' house in Madison," Tovah said. "That must have been the entrance to the root cellar or a storm cellar. That panel is Dave's door to the outside."

She said it with such authority that neither of them felt the need to actually try the route, although Robin did go over and push at one corner of the panel, moving it slightly. A trickle of fresh air answered her gesture.

"Did you know about any of this?" Tovah asked.

Robin sat down on the floor. She pulled up her knees and wrapped her arms around them, making a spot where she could rest her head. "No. No, nothing. I didn't know a thing."

Tovah sat down beside her and put an arm a round Robin's hunched shoulders. Both women had dusty smudges on their faces. They had brushed up against the new construction of the stairwell. Small bits of wood and plaster dust hung suspended in the air.

Tovah sneezed once, then again. "Allergies," she commented. "Let's go back. We need to talk. Don't jump to any conclusions about Dave."

Tovah placed the ladder carefully, resting the front edge against the opening of the trap door. She climbed through, clearly not comfortable with this sort of physical activity. Robin followed. Somehow it seemed the thing to do, rather than taking the regular stairway from the basement to the first floor. It was almost as though they had to prove to themselves that they had actually walked down this secret path from the third floor of the house. They left the ladder standing, a witness. They left the trap door up too, an instinct against getting locked in, the same instinct that had made them so careful before leaving Dave's office. As they walked up the stairs, they again read the book titles of the books above their heads.

"Aha," Tovah said, and she pulled down a black and gold paperback book. Then she took another book, a leather-bound one that looked very old. She selected a few more–small, medium, large–as though choosing by size was as good as any other method of selection.

They emerged from the stairwell feeling like adventurers who had just returned from another planet.

Tovah didn't pay any attention to the neat office they'd returned to, as though it was only a painted backdrop. She dusted her hands on her blue-jeaned thighs, sat down in Dave's big chair, then looked around for a place for Robin to sit. Finding only a small folding chair, she pulled it up close to her own. Robin sat down, falling naturally into the role of student.

Tovah reached over the side of the chair to where she'd stacked the books on the floor. She picked them up and put them on the desk, patting them as though they were animate. "We don't usually put prayer books on the floor," she said to Robin. Then she stood up, as though preparing to deliver a speech.

"Prayer? Dave?" was all Robin could manage to say.

Tovah seemed more comfortable on her feet. She leaned back against the desk, ran her fingers up and down the spines of the books, finally putting her palm flat on the top of the pile.

"Robin," she said, "do you know anything about the Holocaust?" She waited a minute, absorbing Robin's blank stare. "World War II?"

"Of course I know about World War II." Robin shot back, suddenly furious, with Dave and with Tovah too. She could feel her face redden. In a loud, aggravated voice she said, "I went to school the same as you!"

Tovah winced. "Of course you did. But these days you can never know what people learned in school. It's so different around the country."

Robin hastened to apologize. She couldn't believe she had yelled at Tovah. She never yelled at people, never raised her voice. Dave joked that she didn't have a 'loud' button. Her own voice, aggressive and harsh, frightened her, even though it didn't seem to upset Tovah particularly.

The young rabbi held up both her hands, palms out to Robin, a gesture of mollification. "It's okay, no big thing. Look, what we have here is an extensive library of Holocaust literature, and lots of Judaica. Now, I'm sure a Nazi, a neo-Nazi, might have read some of these books, but there's nothing here that isn't authoritative, and I didn't see even one book from the crazies."

Robin knew she looked blank. What was her neighbor trying to tell her?

"Dave is some kind of expert at this, is that what you mean?" Robin's question was tentative. "But, why build this stairway and collect all these books?"

"Well, of course I can't possibly know that. You'll have to talk to Dave." Tovah was thoughtful, evolving some kind of theory, even as she claimed not to know what Dave had been thinking about.

"Obviously he has a deep need to have them, a deep interest in the subject. And if he read and retained everything in these books I guess you could call him an expert. At least he'd be someone who's well up on the history and interpretation of the Holocaust, if not the War itself.

"The Holocaust is the name we give to the destruction of the Jews in Europe. Six million Jews," Tovah concluded.

Robin knew she still must look confused. Her brow furrowed, trying to understand.

The young rabbi tried again. "What I'm saying is: these are not the books of a neo-Nazi. They are the books of a survivor. Or, in Dave's case, and given his age, the child of survivors. It's got to be something like that. The survivors' children usually refer to themselves as the Second Generation.

"This book," she took up a worn-looking paperback volume and held it out to Robin. "It's by Helen Epstein. It's all about them, although it was written a while back."

The name of the pocket book, in gold on black, winked at Robin.

"Dave is too young to be . . . you mean his parents. Do you mean he, they, could be Jews?" Robin said. She thought hard for a minute. "But he never talks about his parents, never. He told me just once, like it was off limits. 'I don't talk about my parents. Just behave as if they never existed.' So I never asked him anything more. I thought maybe they'd died in some horrible way, or that there had been a big fight. You know." Robin felt as though her face had frozen, making it difficult to talk, impossible to smile.

Tovah took several seconds before she responded, clearly considering what Robin had said.

"Well, that's not so uncommon. The children of survivors can be joined to their parents in some death-grip kind of thing. Or, if they couldn't handle it all I guess they might...cut it off. I understand that generally the Second Generation is very protective of their parents. Not that you can cite rules about this. Even if the relationship gets cut off somehow, the arrival of grandchildren usually helps. Did Dave ever want to take Sunny to her grandparents?"

"No, no. You don't think I'd stop him from letting his parents know her? He said once, 'Sunny is her own person, no one else. We'll mess her up enough without another whole generation working at it.'" As they talked Robin felt as a new kind of weight settling on her shoulders, as though forcing her head down. It seemed to her that what they'd just seen, what it all might mean, was too much for her to bear.

After a few seconds, Tovah plowed on. "So what do we do know?" she asked. Fortunately her question was rhetorical, so she didn't wait for an answer. "What's next? Do you want to phone Dave and talk to him? Or do you pretend you didn't see this?"

Robin had to look up to respond. She even had to smile a little. Tovah asked good questions, posing them seriously. They were better, more direct, than many of the questions Robin asked herself.

She stood up, walked toward the files, turned and walked the few steps back across the room to Tovah. "No, I can't pretend any more. I can't ignore this. You might think this is all neat and tidy, that Dave isn't…weird or something. But, I have to know. I can't read through all this at once, but I can look at some of the files. I have to."

Having made a decision, Robin met Tovah's gaze directly; now fierce over the task she'd just set for herself. "I guess I'll have to confront Dave too. But, I can't do that on the phone. I'll have to confirm some things first. The files will help."

"Even just looking through some of the files is going to take a while," Tovah said. "Are you up to it?"

"Well, I don't think I'll sleep much, now."

Robin pulled out each of the drawers of Dave's two file cabinets, one after another. Two were clearly work related, construction bids and contracts. Two others held trip and travel information, files about Dave's summer business. Two of the drawers were empty.

"I'm afraid to look at them," she admitted to Tovah, "and I'm afraid not to."

"That's like Bluebeard's closet. What you might find is worse than not knowing," Tovah said,

"Is that part of what you said before, that this is an annex?" Robin said.

"No, that's a different story. The Annex; well, did you ever read the diary of Anne Frank? Tovah asked cautiously, as though she didn't want to question Robin's knowledge or education again. Then Robin remembered. There was a diary of a teenage girl who had died in one of the concentration camps right at the end of the war. Before she was taken to the camps, she had spent several years with her family hiding in an upstairs apartment built behind a swinging bookcase. *The Diary of a Young Girl* by Anne Frank, had been required reading in eighth grade.

"Is that what you think Dave built here, a secret annex?" Robin would never have thought in those terms.

"It certainly looks like it. If the Franks had been as careful as Dave, they might even have survived in their annex. Of course, Dave had their example to draw from. Otherwise, we wouldn't know what in the hell he was up to."

Both of them were silent, thoughtful, as Robin chose several more files to read, and then locked the cabinets again. The somber expression on Tovah's face told her that her neighbor understood how hard this was for her. Then they filed out of the room, leaving the stairway-bookcase door partially open, as though one of them might want to come back to confirm that it was real. They went down the main stairs of the house, past the safe, pretty bedrooms, to the brightly lit first floor.

CHAPTER TWENTY-ONE

Al Logan's trip to Minneapolis began a few hours after Robin left Sioux Falls. He didn't want to be noticeable, so he didn't take one of the bright red company cars. Instead he rented a large, comfortable Oldsmobile, gray and practically invisible. An Oldsmobile was quite a switch from his younger days, when he'd convinced himself that he needed a motorcycle.

He had to follow Robin. Dave Razkowski wouldn't even allow him in his room. At least Robin was polite. She'd pretend to just be chatting casually, even when she was ducking his questions.

He could afford to be away for a few days. It wasn't a ratings period. The weather–which could be one of the big stories in the Dakotas–continued to be mild and pleasant.

He had all sorts of rationalizations for this trip, but none of them really mattered. His instinct, that this story was important to his future, propelled him more than anything else.

Al hadn't mentioned the climber story at the station for days, not since he'd lost control of Razkowski and Robin.

No one at the station knew his theories about Dave. They'd naturally assumed the story had ended when Al had brought in a short interview and some cute pictures of Sunny with her father.

Who would have guessed that Razkowski would wake up from a coma in less than a week? Who'd have expected a moron like that to take charge?

"Get lost, Logan," he'd said, smiling as though he meant it as a joke, and, as though they had never met before. Al was almost certain that Razkowski remembered him and Rabbi Blumen. But the man never admitted a thing, claimed he didn't remember either of them, didn't remember the whole scene in his room. Wolff Blumen went along with that, seemingly relieved that he didn't have to deal with Dave on an issue like anti-Semitism. No wonder. He and his wife had some cozy deal looking after Razkowski's kid. It made Al sick. The last thing the Blumens needed was one more kid in that tiny house.

He couldn't believe that Dave Razkowski would even let his daughter stay there, a guest in a Rabbi's house. What a story: a neo-Nazi's kid in an Orthodox rabbi's house, while Mommy ran errands for Daddy's sicko organization.

Dave had thrown him out of his room as though Al didn't have the power to get back at him. "Sorry, but we've got a lot of work to do," Dave had said, refusing any kind of lengthy interview, refusing to spend any time with Al. He obviously believed that his own work was the most important thing on earth.

According to Robin, all Dave did was take people back-packing in the summer and do house renovations in the winter. Al smirked. Dave obviously had delusions about his own importance. Unless, the way he made a living was actually a cover up for his real work.

It wouldn't be hard for Razkowski to convince Robin of the importance of his work. He'd already convinced her of other things.

Robin was dumb, yet she wouldn't play along with Al. He'd tried being nice to her, but it was as if she didn't understand his gifts and attention. He couldn't believe that she played the virtuous wife. He'd already ascertained that she was no one's wife at all.

Robin had stood by so loyally when Dave had thrown Al out of his hospital room. She hadn't protested, even though he'd gone out of his way to be nice to her. She'd simply stood with her hand on Dave's shoulder as though they were a Grant Wood painting, a loyal hardworking pair.

Robin had been glad to see the end of him. She hadn't been able to answer his questions. Although she's tried to hid it, it was obvious she didn't know anything about Razkowski's family or about his background. He hadn't set out to make Robin feel dumb or anything, but what else could result if she couldn't answer his simplest questions?

Obviously, he had no choice but to check out the house in Minneapolis. Also, away from Dave, Robin might be more talkative. Once he convinced her it wouldn't take long to gather enough information. This would be a short trip, because Robin wouldn't stay away from her daughter or from Razkowski for too long.

A nurse that he had taken out for lunch had told him about Robin's trip; that she only needed to do one or two things back home: run some errands and collect some paperwork. It seemed likely she was smart enough for that.

So far Al had only a half-formed plan for convincing Robin to talk, for getting into the house. But, his real strength had always been improvisation. He would think of something. He always did.

With Razkowski in a coma from the dumb accident that he'd caused himself, Al hadn't thought Robin would present any kind of a problem. He'd assumed he'd just have to play nice, and to point out that Dave took horrible risks, affecting her well-being and their daughter's life.

But no, Robin insisted she "understood" Dave's actions. Like any strong man, Dave needed to test himself. She'd stared Al down after she said that, daring him to contradict her.

He'd been amazed to hear her say something like that. She must actually believe it. And certainly, she hadn't left him a single opening for a debate.

He could imagine what people in his family—his mother, father and grandmother–would have said about Dave.

"They try to kill us and you want to help them," was what they had said the few times Al undertook anything risky. He couldn't remember the whole list of what was risky, but it included all organized sports, trips out of town, bicycles, and the whole family together in one car, train or plane. The last year he was at home, in high school, it turned out that a motorcycle was the most dangerous of all.

He'd had some money from a small part he'd done with a local theater group. So, he'd bought a motorcycle. He used to feel absolutely sick with fear when he rode it, but in those days he called it excitement.

After a few months he couldn't think of how to get rid of the thing gracefully. He'd finally admitted to himself that it scared him almost as much as it scared the rest of his family. He'd made his point, and he'd got the itch to own a bike out of his system. But he wanted to get rid of it without admitting anything to his family.

Strangely, it was the scholarship he won at the University of Wisconsin that finally let him get rid of the motorcycle. It was also one of the episodes that taught him that you could often win more by upping the odds, then by folding.

He'd told his mother – he'd hated to pick on her, but when it came to the children she was the easiest –he'd decided that the only way he would be able afford school would be if he had cheap transportation. He'd looked at it, he said, and, even with his scholarship, he'd need extra money. He'd need to hold down a job too. So, he was going to take the motorcycle to school, he said. In fact he thought he'd drive it from Boston to Madison.

"He'll be killed!" his mother shrieked at her mother. "All our efforts here and now he'll be killed. And he's the best, the smartest!"

Al didn't pay attention to that part because his mother said that about any child of hers who was trying to do something frightening, or to escape.

His strategy had paid off. He went to college with an allowance and the money for a small car. If hadn't been for the motorcycle he'd have starved at college, trying to survive on the scholarship alone.

Of course the scholarship story looked very different when it was reported in the local newspaper.

His family never showed their problems to the world. Al's mother was always being cited in stories about how well immigrant families did if they had the right values. When the public schools wanted to show off a new American family whose children did well, one of the Lowenthals would be featured.

There would be an explanation of how the family had come to the United States from Hungary. The public version of their story had been highly sanitized, Al later realized. The story always went on to list the activities and accomplishments of Al and all his sisters and brothers. That list included good grades, but also team sports, debating, choirs and amateur theater groups, baby-sitting and other part-time jobs. Al thought that the various ways the six of them had developed to stay out of the bedlam of their house and away from their parents and grandmother showed tremendous ingenuity. The rest of the community thought of it as an innate drive toward excellence and accomplishment.

Secretly, although Al laughed with his brothers and sisters about being 'the best,' he believed that his mother did think of him that way. He was the only one who loved to read as much as she did. He'd studied his mother carefully. He thought he understood what she was attempting and how she set out to accomplish her goals.

Heddy maintained emotional control of her family. If her children didn't follow her direct orders, she had hysterics. If that didn't work, then their grandmother Irene would be sent after them. If the two couldn't bring them into line, then, and only then, it would be up to his father.

Al understood how things worked at home. Maybe he understood because he was the youngest. Maybe it was because by the time he was born his mother's had more time. She'd been rewarded for all her work. She didn't have to go to the barbershop or the beauty salon any more. She could do as she liked. It turned out that what she liked was to lie on her bed twenty hours out of every day and read.

Once he was grown, Al figured that the best times of his life had been the hours spent with his mother and her books, hours of reading. His mother and her books were a wonderful help in school and in college, probably more responsible for his exceptionally high verbal SAT scores than anything that he had ever learned in school. Al figured it was his good luck that his mother had brains along with her beauty.

His father's and his grandmother's desires didn't encompass English literature, but they were quite a pair in their own way

Al called them Boris and Natasha, from the Bullwinkle show. Even Heddy laughed at that.

"But this Natasha," his mother would say, her Hungarian accent giving English elegant flourishes it didn't otherwise possess. "She looks more like me, your Natasha. More. Than. Like. Your. Grand. Mother."

Heddy often said words that were important to her as if they were separate sentences. "Your. Grand. Mother."

Boris and Natasha were his father and grandmother. What a pair they must have been before they were old and used up.

They said that they had planned the life they'd wanted, that they'd achieved, while still in the camps. How could that have been possible? But, they'd insisted that in the camps everyone knew that after the war they would need money to be safe, and children. Money and children were survival.

Their belief in a future had kept them alive in the camps. You had to believe in something in order to survive.

Al had to hand it to them. Where ever they had been when they planned it, they accomplished what they set out to do: six kids and three businesses.

And all of it, at least the beginning, had happened because his mother Heddy had been taught to cut hair in the DP camps.

Al used to joke that if she'd been taught welding instead of barbering in the Displaced Persons camps, then his family might have ended up owning steel mills, or they might have been a ring of safe-crackers.

He couldn't help but be proud of them. Their accomplishments weren't bad for two old people to whom the most important thing in the world, the WAR, had happened in the mid 1940's, years before his birth. Nothing in their life matched up to the War in importance, but they worked hard anyway. Al couldn't figure them out at all. Most of the time, he didn't even try.

It just seemed to Al that he had three parents—mother, father and grandmother—and that not one of them would actually tell any of the children what had happened to them during the War.

None of this had been on Al's mind for years and years. Now it was all he could think about. It was Wolff Blumen's fault. Damn him. Damn the maddening questions that he didn't actually ask, that just seemed to peer out, unspoken, from those dark, brown eyes.

Damn him, too, for knowing so exactly how Al felt.

Al damned Wolff and he cursed Dave Razkowski and his dumb blonde, Robin. Right now she likely felt so safe, tucked away in her snazzy, immaculate, totally redone house. All he'd wanted was for Robin to see Dave as he did.

He'd find a way to get what he wanted from her. He glanced into the back seat of the car. He had Dave's cut-away boot and the axe, the things he'd conveniently kept 'forgetting' to bring to Robin at the hospital. He couldn't imagine how he would put his ideas and the props together, but he would think of something.

He needed this story. He could work himself into a fine white-hot fury over a story like this, and do something creative with it. He lived for this kind of story.

Al reached Minneapolis and drove to Razkowski's address. It was an ordinary urban street of older houses. He recognized the house right away from Robin's description. After he'd reconnoitered carefully he parked a discreet distance away.

He saw it right away: she was nervous. The first and second floors of her house blazed with light.

As he sat in the car he saw a neighbor lady hurry over, carrying a plate wrapped in tin foil.

That must be the rabbi-neighbor that Robin had talked about. When he'd quizzed Robin about Dave she'd talked about lots of other things, continually changing the subject to get away from his questions. For some reason Robin was proud of having a neighbor who was a rabbi. She seemed to think of it as especially classy. The rabbi must finally be making some sort of token social call. Robin had suggested they hardly knew each other, so they wouldn't have much to say. He could wait.

He watched lights go on even farther back in the house. They must be eating, drinking coffee. After awhile, there was a light on the third floor too.

Al had to shift his position in the car. He checked his watch. It was getting too late for him to just drop by. He'd have to come back.

Just then, the third floor light went off and seconds later he saw the door to the porch open. The two women stood on the stairs of the house, talking.

This was his moment! As if his cue had just sounded, as if a footlight had just illuminated his stage, Al's scene began. He pulled out of his parking space, blessing the fact that he was far enough down the tree-lined street to be invisible to the women.

He wheeled into the driveway right behind Dave's Wrangler.

"Hey!" he called as he emerged from the car, all energy and good intentions. "Good! I was just zipping by so I'd know where to go in the morning. I just got in. I've got some of Dave's stuff in the car, the stuff I liberated from that Ranger who brought it in. I wanted to be sure you got it back, so I thought I'd take this opportunity. So you wouldn't have to worry about getting it home from Sioux Falls."

Robin frowned. She looked surprised and not at all pleased to see him.

"Well." He smiled broadly. "You have more company!"

He offered his hand to the other woman. After all, meeting a neighbor had to be the most ordinary thing in the world.

He directed his own actions as he improvised: use the friendly hearty handshake and the voice and serve up a big smile with the introduction.

"Al Logan," he said.

"Tovah Feldner."

Al turned to Robin. "Your neighbor?"

"Rabbi Feldner." Robin said stone-faced, voice flat.

What was wrong? Could she really so angry that he'd showed up in Minneapolis? He didn't think that was it. She kept looking up: *Why? Not up at the sky. No, it's the house. What is up there? And there's no smile at all, not even just with the lips.*

Something had happened to these two. Something had happened up there, or they'd both seen something. But what?

He certainly didn't let them know what he was thinking. "Let me give you Dave's stuff and get out of here. I thought it was way too late to stop, but I'm glad I spotted you. I've got important meetings tomorrow, downtown, so I've got a room at the Marriot. I have such a bad sense of direction though. I thought I'd save getting lost tomorrow; just do it tonight instead. I always get lost. I know men aren't supposed to admit that."

Al had to laugh at his own joke. They weren't going to do it.

He went on, "I don't have your home phone number. I thought that I might miss you tomorrow, if I got lost. Then I'd have to tote the stuff back or just leave it and hope you'd get it okay. I meant to give it to you, remember? But, Dave surprised us all and woke up so soon."

He couldn't figure out what was going on with these women. It seemed to him that these two were shell-shocked. Now he really had to get inside the house.

They stood on the stairs watching him, one blonde and one brunette, both looking like hypnotized watchdogs. You just do your thing, Al told himself, as he turned to get Dave's things from his car.

By the time he returned the Rabbi was saying she ought to go, although she didn't actually leave.

Mutely, as though turning over treasure, Al offered Robin the climbing axe that he'd acquired in the parking garage. For the moment he'd left Dave's boot in the car.

"I thought this looked valuable…and lethal, at least to me. I'm sure Dave knows what to do with it."

He paused for a second. "I've got to call and tell the hotel to hold my room and my cell phone has run down. The station hates when I make casual calls. They claim it costs them a fortune. If that's true, I don't think much of their plan. If these phones were so expensive they wouldn't be catching on the way they are. Can I use your phone?"

Robin took the axe. "You said you also had his boot?"

"Did I forget that again?" Al said in an absent-minded way. He brushed past Robin as she stood to one side in the open doorway. His manner established that permission to use the phone had either been given or could be assumed.

"Where?" he asked.

"It's in the kitchen, at the back." She pointed.

He walked slowly down a long hall toward the back of the house. The usual: living room, family room, dining room, one after another. At the back of the house there was a brand new kitchen with an informal eating area beyond the work area. Two yellow, white and blue flowered mugs, used napkins, and small, bright yellow plates with crumbs on them stood on the round table.

Al hollered, "Found it" toward the front of the house as he picked up the phone.

"Can I use your can?" he called out to Robin as he pretended to punch in a phone number. He stepped out into the hall and waved at Robin.

"There's a bathroom back there," she said. He voice sounded calm enough, but her body moved jerkily. She threw a glance toward the other woman, but Al couldn't see the rabbi's reaction.

He walked through the kitchen into the back hall and found the bathroom. He'd created a few precious minutes for himself, and he intended to use them to insure that he would be able to get back into the house later that night. Quickly and quietly he snapped open the lock on the back door of the house and stuffed wadded up toilet paper into the setting for the bolt to make sure it stayed open. He could count on the fact that she'd never check, because she knew the door was already locked.

He walked through the house to the front door.

"Thanks," he said. "I'm glad I was able to phone from here. I'd hate not to have a place to stay at this time of night, especially with an early morning meeting."

He walked between his car and the Jeep then opened the door. "You must be exhausted," he said. "I am. It's quite a ride. I should have thought of it sooner; we could have come in together. Oh, it's been very nice to meet you, Rabbi." He slid into the car, deliberately 'forgetting' Dave's boot.

He made sure they saw the lights of his car as he pulled up to the closest corner and turned, heading back to Hennepin Ave and, they would assume, to his downtown hotel.

Al didn't return to Robin's neighborhood for several hours. He could be somewhat patient now that he'd fixed the door. It was well past midnight when he parked down the block again. Now the house was almost completely dark. There was only one light on, at the front of the house. Probably she'd kept a light on in her bedroom. After all, she was alone.

Was she still awake, or asleep with the lights on?

He'd have to wait. He could afford to wait, even though being alone had become more difficult than it had ever been in the past. He'd wait until she had to be asleep. Then he'd get inside to see exactly what had spooked the two women. Meantime he could doze, try to avoid the questions that ran through his head these days.

–That rabbi. The questions were really his. He didn't actually ask them, but they came anyway, as though Blumen's careful listening brought the questions into being.

–Your mother survived on the streets of Budapest alone, at that age, without anyone to help her?

–She was with Wallenberg, as a runner?

Wolff didn't say that Wallenberg had only been active there for a few months before the Russians got him. He didn't ask: What did she do the rest of the time?

–What did she have to do to survive?

–And with whom?

–Exactly how old was she?

Al concentrated on the last question, always a source of humor, even in his humorless family. How old? A Hungarian woman never tells anyone her age.

What did her real age matter? His mother possessed great beauty, the real thing. He'd always tried to do what she wanted him to do, to make her happy. She deserved to be happy. She'd had a hard life: the War, the communists, then the DP camps and a new country. During the war her mother had been taken away and her father and brother had died.

Al couldn't actually tell his mother how much he cared about what had happened to her. She must know that it was the most important thing in his life. When he was young he'd kept 'dangerous' activities down to a minimum, just for her.

The most dangerous thing he'd ever done was the surgery in Mexico. God knows what they did to you once you were out cold during a procedure, or even just heavily doped up, as he'd been.

His mother had known right away that he'd had plastic surgery. She's realized it the moment she saw him. But she only knew after it was all over.

She'd run her hand over the line of his jaw then traced the same line on her own face. She didn't say anything. He could tell that her eyes were memorizing the new contours of his face, so she could continue to compare them with her own.

She'd have done it, too. If surgery could have saved her, she'd have done it. Since he'd gone on TV she'd never asked him too many questions. She'd never said a word to him about the surgery. His father and his grandmother hadn't seemed to notice.

When Al finally awoke it was well after three a.m. Robin was sure to have fallen asleep.

He'd been dreaming about his family. The dream had left a strange tangle of familiar images in his head, old family photos mixed up with people like Robin and Rabbi Blumen. All the people kept combining and re-combining in strange ways, as though their different family reunions had become confused.

He pushed the images aside in the same way he would have put away a family photograph album, telling himself that there were more important things to do right now. He could think about all of that later. His dreams meant nothing. Those strange combinations of people and images were just the result of dozing off while remembering the doctor's reaction to the pictures of his mother and grandmother. His surgery had been done four years ago. In all that time, he'd never again thought about that moment with the doctor. So, how important could it be?

"Time to go to work," he said out loud, like a director speaking to an actor. He glanced up at the house. The light in the bedroom was still on, although it seemed dimmer. Al made a bet with himself: even-odds she'd decided to sleep with a light on as insurance against things that go bump in the night. Well, he'd be there, but there would be no bump, no trace, unless he wanted to leave it.

He made Robin nervous. He knew that. It pleased him. The idea that he didn't bother her at all would have troubled him far more than the fact that he upset her.

He wanted her upset, off guard, disturbed. As far as he was concerned, she deserved it. But, right now she could sleep. He wanted to see what she'd seen, to know what had upset her and her neighbor. From her hostile reaction just seeing him, he'd finally given up on the idea that he might get her on his side. He'd get his story in a more direct way.

He picked up a nylon backpack with his video camera inside. He slung the pack over his shoulder, wanting his hands free. But then, on impulse, he took the pack off. He removed the camera and shoved what he thought of as his last prop, Dave's boot, inside. He hadn't decided yet, but maybe he'd leave it on the porch when he was finished, to spook Robin.

He probably would never be able to get away with a shot that actually identified the house. But there was always the chance that something indistinct, taken at night through the trees, would get past the lawyers. If this story ever aired someone in Minneapolis would recognize where the picture had been taken. That would serve Razkowski right. And, the fact that the trees were starting to lose their leaves would establish the time of the year, no matter when the story appeared.

Al slipped down the alley behind the house and circled around the back of the garage. He held his breath as he tried the back door. He didn't want the lock to snap shut so first he inserted the old reliable, a credit card.

Once inside he swung the camera up to his shoulder and shot video footage as he walked to the front of the house and up the stairs. Razkowski had done a good job. The stairs, carpeted in gray Berber, were silent. He stopped at the room where the light shone. It had to be the master bedroom. In his perfect fantasy-drama he would have been gutsy enough to crack the door just a little and get an image of Robin asleep, maybe reflected in a mirror. Far better for him to imagine that kind of thing though, rather then mess up while attempting it. He would never be that foolhardy. In all likelihood Robin would be sleeping very lightly. She'd been very upset when he'd last seen her.

Damn! The stairs to the third floor weren't carpeted. He walked gingerly, staying to the outside of the treads. Stairs made less noise that way.

By the time he had gained the third floor, his script was developing, with him as the hero, undercover style. He kept the camera rolling. It had a very sensitive light setting that guaranteed him an image under almost any circumstances. He had no idea if he'd ever be able to use this footage, but, right now, he had the view of the world that he liked best, through a camera lens.

Once he got to the third floor things were not what he'd expected.

First of all, he met resistance when he tried to enter Dave's office. It felt as though something blocked the doorway. How in the hell had Robin and her neighbor got themselves out of the office, with something planted in front of the door? Finally the door yielded to an especially energetic push. But, he'd been frozen for a second or two before he'd risked it. What if they'd left a booby trap to catch him? Was it possible that the police were involved?

Even at first glance Al could see that the office was all wrong. Razkowski didn't have any weird war memorabilia on display. There were no Nazi battle flags, no pictures with the wrong people as heroes. In Al's experience most guys with Fascist leanings liked to show off that sort of thing, at least in their private spaces. Well, Razkowski might not do that, not with the neighbors he had.

If Razkowski's office housed any spooky stuff, it certainly wasn't obvious. He'd never seen such an ordinary office. He scanned the portion he'd seen first in his view-finder: desk, computer, pens and pencils in a large mug, two regulation gray, metal, four-drawer file cabinets. They were ordinary commercial cabinets, but the drawers were protected with specially installed locks. That might be significant. Al honed in on them with his camera. If he needed it later he would have a shot that implied that there was something questionable inside. He could always cut away to papers or objects to suggest that he'd had access to those locked drawers. He'd have to think about what the contents might be.

The books open on the desk, some of them open, might be important. He let his camera's eye record them, one at a time. Through the viewer of the camera he read: *Children of the Holocaust Children of Survivors of the Holocaust Tell Their Stories.* He knew that book; he had it in his own locked-up library.

An old prayer book, all Hebrew, a European publisher, came next. The third book was Lucy Davidovicz's *The War Against the Jews*, an early authoritative history about the Nazi death machine. It had a whole section on the invasion of Hungary. It had been one of the first serious history books Al had ever read.

Next, to his amazement, he found a small book, just like one his mother owned. It was something so precious to her that she'd only let the children look at it under her direct supervision. The book had only been given to Displaced Persons who had managed to gain visas to the U.S. It told potential immigrants what they might expect to find in the United States. Al's mother's copy was in English and Hungarian. This copy was in Polish, Yiddish and English. It had been printed on cheap paper that was now crumbling. Al kept his camera trained on it. With his free hand he turned a few of the ragged pages, his fingers gentle, the way his mother had always insisted that this particular book had to be handled.

He watched his own hand, confused by what he felt and saw. Had Robin set him up in some way? How had all this come about?

The flood of emotions, the confusion that coursed through him, became so acute that he had to turn away. The camera swung aimlessly, bobbed around, as though trying to find another place to fix its attention, some image that wouldn't be so disturbing.

Through the viewfinder, Al saw an oddly placed, very deep bookcase next to the door. It must have been what had partially blocked his entrance into the room. It stood not quite – but almost – at a right angle to the wall. He began to move toward the bookcase, and only then realized that the bookcase was out of place. It belonged flat against the wall, beside the door. At almost the same moment he also realized that he'd almost stepped into a narrow, black rectangle of open space at his feet.

He jumped back. Then, slowly, he moved closer to the edge. His fingers worked instinctively, flipping on the small, strong light attached to his camera. Now he wanted all the light he could get.

A clean white set of stairs rolled away from him, illuminated for the camera, for his eyes. Each tread had a safety strip that gleamed back at him like the eyes of a thousand small animals trapped in a cellar.

His body responded before his brain did, interpreting his surprise in strong physical sensations. The charge was immediate, sexual, beginning in his groin and moving up through his body. He could feel the hairs on his forearms, and on the back of his neck stir. His pulse and his breathing went into over-drive, even though he continued to stand absolutely still.

Then he stepped back, adjusted the light, and let it play along the walls of the space. He saw a light fixture, but ignored it. He saw several rows of books beneath his feet and then, suddenly, they were above his head. He was half a flight down the stairs, even though he'd had no conscious thought of starting in that direction. He turned back to look up at the opening to this stairwell. Just like Alice-down-the-rabbit-hole.

Turning again, his camera played lower down on the walls. He saw food, and more food, arrayed along shelves in rows, freeze-dried packages stacked up and staples stored in immaculate glass jars. The basics of life were arrayed before him; food and water, some medicines, cleaning supplies. On one side the banister served to lock many of the containers in place. Other shelves had a safety lip, but most were secured with black cord. Al reached his left hand into the camera's viewing territory, while his right held the camera steady against his shoulder. The black cords were elastic. His fingers strummed them. They were secured to hooks set into the studs of the house and to the uprights of the shelves. He could hear the faint thrumming of the bungee cords, like bees, like modern music he had heard somewhere.

If only he could have recorded his own face at that moment, twisted in the expression of shock he knew to be there. This place was about the purest of motives, survival and self-defense. This was what people like me, the children of Holocaust survivors, are driven to.

And so, finally, with his instincts operating and his prejudices pushed aside, Al knew Dave's story.

His left hand looked huge in the viewfinder of the camera. Somewhere in the back of his totally shocked brain he recognized a great shot, a link to the shot with the books upstairs on the desk. He would find the atonal music that had come to mind, and use it as background to this story. When the whole world was out of tune, you needed music to match.

He knew it was his hand that was visible, but somehow it had very little to do with him. Rather, it had to do with the story he was going to create. It had already become part of the show. That hand would make the details of the story more poignant, even though he wasn't entirely sure yet what those details might be.

He shifted the camera angle up, up, up, flipping a lens so that he could see what was stored at the top. After seeing those books on Dave's desk, he wasn't surprised to be standing at the bottom of an exceptional library. He'd read many of these books himself. He owned some of them, keeping them carefully locked up with his survival gear, where no one, not even his cleaning lady, ever saw it. Elie Wiesel, Martin Gilbert, Paul Johnson; these were all books by a well-known authors who had written significant, authoritative books about the Holocaust. Razkowski even had the complete set of the atlases that showed every significant troop and train movement of World War ll. Al had looked at that matched set of volumes himself, but he'd had to defer actually purchasing it. He didn't have room for anything like that.

The jolt of recognition he'd felt when he'd first seen the material in Dave's office rocketed through him again, stronger, harder. Like Al, Dave Razkowski's private world revolved around secrecy. Their methods were radically different, but their goals were identical, privacy equaling protection.

He felt compelled to admire Dave's efforts, so far beyond his own. The man who had designed this space was an artist. This facility Razkowski had created, that he must have built by himself, was light-years beyond his own locked-up closet full of books and an emergency suitcase.

He'd have to start all over with Razkowski's story, but now it would be easy; a gift. He would be telling his own story too. He could have built this facility. One day he'd have something like this, but it would be classy, not so obvious.

Al could already see himself debating the idea of a bunker–this bunker–with Dave: Was it smart to be so immobile? You could be given up for some cheesy reward, for extra food, or immunity. Something like that had happened to the Frank family and to other families Al knew about.

Good! He would make that debate part of his show. He could argue both sides. On one side: you had to make a stand somewhere. That would probably be Dave's argument. Al could concede that he might be right. But, Al could also coolly point out; what if the situation became truly hopeless? Then, how could anything save you?

When he presented the story, he would be sympathetic, but clinical. No one would ever know how the subject affected him personally.

Later, Al would ask himself how he knew so quickly, instinctively really, what all the important elements were? Certainly, he didn't find what he'd come after. But, eventually he would be able to concede, at least to himself, that he knew the story because it was his own. He understood the bunker as the response of a man who needed to save himself and his family should some Neo-Nazi group ever come to power and want to finish the job that had been started in the middle of the century. If that happened, Al planned to save himself, too.

Al had asked his father once, just once, right before he'd left for college, how it was that he had survived when so many others didn't. "Because I was strong," his father had said. Al had looked around at his mother, at his grandmother. They were all sitting together for once, watching television. He could tell that the women didn't believe what his father had just said.

His grandmother said, "It could just be good luck to survive. Sometimes it could even be bad luck to survive. The price to survive could be very high, even too high."

Al didn't understand that answer, but he knew very clearly when his parents or his grandmother closed a subject.

His mother had stood up and gone to her bedroom, back to her stacks of library books. His grandmother had looked at his father in that way the two of them had, a way that Al had never understood. They'd left the living room together. They would have gone to the kitchen or the decrepit office next to it, where everything reeked of his father's cigars. They would drink tea and work on the books of the barbershop, the beauty parlor or the cleaning service. Or, they would go to one of the two shops to clean up and prepare for the next day. They might just sit and talk, making elaborate plans for the next business they wanted to start. That's what they always did.

Suddenly, standing on the second landing of Dave Razkowski's stairwell, Al realized that it was his grandmother and his father who were the real couple in his family, not his mother and his father. He sat down on the stairs, stunned. For the first time, he ignored the camera, even though the slight vibration on his shoulder still served as background. His face twisted. He'd never asked for this insight. What was he supposed to do with it? But, how could he have missed it: his father and his grandmother.

What did that mean? His mother was the beauty in the family, and sometimes the brains. She had been the youth and strength when that was necessary, like in the DP camps. She'd been the only one young enough to be trained to do something. They'd taught her to cut hair. She'd learned the rest later, long before Al was born, but after they'd come to Boston: his mother Heddy, his father Anatoly, his grandmother Irene and his eldest brother and sister, Sandor and Victoria. The other children had been born in Boston. So, his grandmother had been too old to have children. Maybe she'd been hurt too badly during the war? Al's face contorted to keep tears from falling.

How could he never before realized that his father had come to Hungary after the war to find his grandmother, not her daughter?

When his grandmother had been in the camps, she must have thought that her daughter was dead, just like her son. The fact that Heddy had survived must have been a shock. If any marriage had been dreamed about in Auschwitz, it wouldn't have been for Irene, not Heddy.

But children were so important after the war. Al had heard that all his life. His fists tightened reflexively when he thought of what they must have done to his grandmother in the camps, what might have prevented her from ever bearing more children. Or maybe she was just too old? His mind couldn't grasp the arithmetic of his family's history. All he knew was that whatever the reason, the children they'd all wanted so badly after the war could only come from Heddy's body.

The family story had always said that the marriage was to protect Heddy. That had a ring of truth about it. It had been repeated time after time. The children had assumed that the marriage had been to protect Heddy from the dangerous times after the war, when Hungary became Communist.

But, he must always have known they didn't mean that. It was just that with all the turmoil following the war, it was hard to believe that the fate of one youngster who had been out on the streets, prostituting herself in order to live, had actually mattered.

Al thought he would throw up. Deep in his heart he knew that his mother had survived as a prostitute. Worse, he'd known it most of his life.

It meant that Heddy had consorted with enemy soldiers; that she had 'fraternized.' Al's stomach knotted in response to the first flush of anger that realization brought with it. Rigorously he suppressed that feeling within. He knew that he would have done what she had done, and more, to survive. He was just like her.

At that moment he was glad he had decided to face the world without the drag of his family. He would never be able to face his mother again, no matter how much he loved her. But, at the same time, he would never be able to forget, or push this knowledge aside. And his own face, modeled so closely on hers, would be his daily reminder.

Al sat slumped on the stairs of Dave's bunker. It was as though the reality of Dave's creation all around him had required truth from him, too. For the moment he forgot how he had gained entry to this place, that he should still concern himself with being caught.

He stood up, summoning every ounce of energy to continue down the stairs. He didn't need anything more from Dave.

The camera resting on his shoulder recalled itself; its vibration travelling through him. It modulated into the one feeling in the world that he trusted. The excitement, the white-hot feeling that told him this couldn't miss. White Hot!

There, he had it. He had more than a story. He had a whole series. It would be a series of stories of the same intensity as this one, all white hot stories. *White Hot!* That was it.

For his first show he'd restage this whole bunker. His retelling would say: Look at a whole generation affected. See what children of such trauma are driven to do in order to survive.

The story would illustrate their toxic inheritance; fear transmuted as though through the genes.

He didn't need Dave Razkowski at all to tell this story. He didn't even need the images he'd just captured, although they would guide him. He would tell this story his own way, from his own experience.

Al's own family had chosen survival, no matter what the cost. He, too, would choose survival and success. He would pay any price required.

Slowly at first, heavy with his new burden, he began walking down the stairs. But then, careless of the details of the careful construction around him, and careless about keeping silent, he began to move faster.

CHAPTER TWENTY-TWO

obin had fallen asleep on a bed littered with the files she'd taken from Dave's office. What she'd read ought to have appeared in her dreams, but maybe it was all too new. Rather, she seemed to be in a gym on a Stairmaster, never been her favorite workout machine. But she was obliged to climb on, even though the machine made a strange noise. Then, in her dream, she couldn't reach the switch to turn it off. The more effort she made, the more the action speeded up, the further away the switch.

"Aha," Robin told herself in her dream. "I bet it thinks I'm not smart enough to figure this out. If it moves away and speeds up when I work harder, I'll just slow down."

In her dream, she did that. The machine slowed down. The switch moved closer. She felt a moment of exhilaration at her triumph of logic, but it was short-lived, even by disturbing-dream standards. As the Stairmaster slowed down it somehow began to enclose her, as if it shrunk around her. Now she couldn't move her arms, so she still couldn't turn off the machine. She would never be able to step off.

The machine had become a pair of arms now, the arms of someone who had clamped his arms around the upper part of her body. She was pressed tight against a man. His body was insistent, sexually charged. She could feel him, hard against the crease of her buttocks. She struggled and tried to wrench free. What if it was Dave? But she had to get free!

Then, suddenly, she awoke, finding herself sitting upright in her bed. It was as though the struggle had left her gasping for air. A small light was still on and the radio played very softly.

She shook her head slightly to clear the dream away. But one part of it, the insistent, repetitive sound of the Stairmaster did not stop.

In a second she realized that the noise came from the stairwell. Footsteps; was it Dave?

Of course it wasn't Dave.

Robin levered herself out of bed. Still dressed, but without shoes, without a thought of what she might find, she tore up the stairs to Dave's office.

Once there she felt oddly disoriented for a moment. She remembered very clearly that she and Tovah had edged out of the office. They hadn't wanted to move the bookcase back into place. Now there was a lot more space than when they'd left the room.

The borrowed glow of a street lamp illuminated the main features of the room a little, but the illumination was still low enough to show that there was also a light moving in the stairwell.

Later, Robin would be hard-pressed to believe that she had been so brave, or so foolhardy. But without thinking she lowered herself into the stairwell.

She tried for first light on her way down, but her fingers only grazed it. She concentrated on hitting the next light, not wanting to face who ever she'd find in darkness.

She could see almost straight down into the bottom of the stairwell despite the curve built in toward the bottom. There was a figure on the stairs between her and the trap door that she and Tovah had left raised earlier that evening. The person ahead of her reached the bottom of the stairs and turned to climb down the ladder. A beam of light swept up the stairs and caught her full in the face, a blow from an unexpected hand.

He or she negotiated the ladder cautiously. Robin heard the slower careful steps. Then, after a second or two of silence, she heard the noisy clatter of feet on the regular basement stairs up to the first floor. She'd made it all the way to the bottom by then. She pushed the ladder aside and dropped through the trap, ducking her head. Otherwise she would hit the low ceiling that formed the bottom of Dave's secret stairwell. She hurried to follow the intruder up the basement stairs. When she got to the first floor back hallway she flipped on the lights. The back door gaped open. Robin drew in a deep breath, readying herself to pursue the intruder. She had a good chance to catch him. But something tangled around her feet as she crossed the back landing and she was sent sprawling. Her lungs emptied as though they were squeezed bellows and she cracked her elbow on the front edge of the outside stairs. It was such an exquisitely painful injury all she could manage to do once she pulled herself upright was cradle the injured part of her body. Her intruder escaped.

Still gasping for air, she sat on the back stairs of her house. The night sky was velvet, dark blue and without a cloud. The stars, washed out by the lights of the city, were feeble and far away. The pain in her elbow receded a little. She flexed it, slowly and carefully, her fingers checking for damage. Behind the pain her mind was perfectly clear.

How could she ever have believed that she didn't have a stake here? This was hers too, this porch, even that stairway. She had a right and a responsibility toward all of it, just as Dave did.

She reached back for whatever had tripped her and found a nylon backpack.

Inside she found a new, wrapped, professional videotape cassette and a boot, Dave's boot. The boot that had been cut away by the rescue worker's who'd saved him. Her fingers traced where the sharp instrument had followed exactly on the line of a seam, cutting the stitches but not the leather. It actually looked as though it could be mended.

Disgusted, Robin flung the boot in the general direction of the trash. She would not allow Dave to even think about getting the boot fixed, then using it for the same kind of trip. Whether he knew it yet or not, those days were over!

And, of course, the boot confirmed exactly who had been in the stairwell. Sitting there on her back stairs, her breathing slowly returning to normal, her elbow throbbing, her clothes gritty and dirty against her body, Robin knew: Al Logan.

She suddenly felt very calm, the kind of calm that is next door to total despair. The situation had become so much more complicated than anything she could have imagined. There was no way to know what Al Logan would do with the information he now had. She would have to tell Dave, and that would be the end of them as a couple, as a family.

She rose slowly and re-entered the house. When she tried to lock the door she felt resistance to the bolt turning. Once she'd examined the back door lock she knew exactly how Al got in. It had been so easy. He hadn't even had to steal the key they kept hidden up high, near the back door. It was still there, another one of Dave's careful plans. Dave had so many complicated, sophisticated plans to keep everyone safe, and they had all failed.

She was surprised by her own calm. In fact, her surprise was stronger than any other emotion.

She had work to do tomorrow, meetings to attend with Dave's experts. She went upstairs, dropped her clothes on the bathroom floor, and took a quick shower. Then, with the lights out and the radio off, she went back to bed and slept until the alarm woke her in the morning.

PART THREE

Isaac Liberated

The text says that Abraham returned from Moriah but omits a mention of Isaac. Is it possible that Isaac did not come back with his father, that the trauma of near-death tore the taut strings that bound the son to the father?

Gleanings: The Akedah (The Binding of Isaac)
Genesis 22:1-24

The Five Books of Moses: A Modern Commentary
By Rabbi W. Gunther Plaut

CHAPTER TWENTY-THREE

It was Wednesday afternoon before Robin could force herself to return to Sioux Falls, even though Sunny was waiting for her, even though Dave's business had been concluded on Monday. By the time she'd met Jess and heard all that he had to say she was exhausted, beyond her wildly interrupted night's sleep, beyond the discoveries she and Tovah had made. Plus, she'd barely made a dent in the pile of Dave's files that she needed to read.

Tovah, and her husband Dan Goldin, invited her to dinner on Monday and she went, grateful for the distraction, for the chatter of the children. Doing things as ordinary as setting the table for Tovah's burrito dinner was so comforting. The two women called back and forth to each other as they worked.

When they all sat down to eat, Dan said, "I think you ought to stay in town another day at least, Robin. You look like you've been through the mill."

Dan was exotically handsome. At one time Robin would have been mortified if such a good looking man had said something like that to her, but she could tell there was no criticism implied here, only concern.

Dan was right. On Tuesday Robin felt worse. She pulled herself out of bed and called Dave, using the only excuse that came to mind.

"I think I have the flu. I don't think I can drive today."

She called Faiga too, to explain why she wasn't back yet. She was only a little more straightforward with her friend than she'd been with Dave. "Things have been... It's hard to explain over the phone. I know your holidays start soon. I'll be back tomorrow."

"*Rosh Hashanah* begins Friday night, so there's time," Faiga said. "You sound exhausted. Maybe you ought to take another day."

On Wednesday morning Tovah came over for a hasty visit. Robin had closed both entrances to Dave's annex by then, carefully replacing everything in his office. Neither woman referred to the structure directly, although both were acutely aware of it, a presence hovering over and around them. Twice during their conversation, as they sat over coffee in the kitchen, Tovah gestured toward a wall as though she could see through it into the annex beyond.

"Are you sure you can drive that distance, Robin?" What are you going to say to Dave? He hasn't really done anything harmful or..."

"I have no idea what I'm going to say to him," Robin admitted. She'd shared a little of the information in the files with Tovah. She'd spent most of the evening before reading the file, Razkowski, J. That was Dave's father, Jacob. He had been interned in a Nazi labor camp at fifteen. He'd been transferred from one work camp to another, a litany of horrors. He'd been a slave laborer in a salt mine in Poland, then he'd been sent to a brutal lumber camp. He'd ended up in the Bergen-Belsen death camp. Amazingly, he had survived it all. He'd barely been in his twenties at the end of war when he was finally liberated.

Feldefing, the name on another of Dave's files, and on a small book Robin had found in the annex, had been a Displaced Person's camp in post-World War ll Europe. Dave's parents had met there and married. Dave's older brother had been born there, too. Despite reading the files and Tovah's insistence, Robin still had trouble believing that that those long-time-ago events were the reason Dave had built his staircase-annex.

Once Robin was on the road back to Sioux Falls she realized she wasn't concentrating on her driving at all. There was only one major turn to make, onto I-90 West, and she almost missed it. Great, all she needed was to be in a car accident, to be useless to herself, to Sunny, and to Dave too. Angrily, she punched the button on the tape player to provide some company. She had one of her old aerobics tapes in the tape deck. Disco music blared in her ears. That was a big mistake. It was the tape she'd used a lot around the time she'd first met Dave.

Her boss at the health club in Fargo had always insisted that the girls on staff sell memberships to the men who joined the club. That was how she'd met Dave.

He'd been interested in the steam room, the weights and the pool, but dismissive of the aerobics studio. "Very nice," he'd said, "But it's for the ladies."

For some reason, she'd wanted this man to take what she did for a living seriously. "I bet you wouldn't think it was just for the ladies if you tried my ninety minute Sunday morning Super Aerobics class. I bet I could floor you," she said. She'd tapped the bright blue resilient floor in the studio with the toe of her sneaker, as though in a dare.

The class had been her idea. Her boss had even paid her a cash bonus because she'd made the class into one of the hot singles spots in Fargo.

Dave showed up the very next Sunday and seemed to be keeping up just fine. As soon as they'd met she'd know that he was in great shape. At the end of the class he had stayed in the studio. As she walked over to find out what he wanted, he'd suddenly collapsed. She'd raced over to where he lay on the floor. She'd wanted to impress him, not kill him. He was lying there, grinning up at her. "Okay, you floored me," he'd said. "Now you'll have to go out to brunch with me, to help me recover."

That memory was so poignant she actually had to pull over to the side of the highway. But, if she stopped every time she remembered something like that she'd never get to Sioux Falls. With extra determination Robin took a new hold on the steering wheel and eased back into traffic, blinking away her tears and clearing her throat as though preparing to speak to Dave at that moment.

Oddly, what was foremost in her mind just then wasn't facing Dave, or even talking to him about what she'd found at home. Even the issue of Al Logan was far from her mind. Instead, she found herself trying to reconstruct her history with Dave. Did all his secrets make it something new? What had she missed in all those years of living with the man that she loved?

Dave always said he was an ordinary Joe, a 'six pack and lunch bucket guy.' She'd always known that wasn't true. Dave's intelligence and complexity were things she loved. Before this she'd always assumed that he had reasons she didn't fully understand for the things, for the things he did that she found incomprehensible.

Certainly Dave's reasons for leaving Fargo had never been clear to her. One day he had never mentioned moving, the next he had an army of logical excuses as to why they ought to leave.

"I've decided that Fargo isn't the right base for a wilderness business," he'd said one morning in April, still winter in North Dakota. "People have to travel too far to get here. Then I drag them even further, to the site."

Robin had been clearing the breakfast table and she stopped with her hands full of dirty dishes. "But you have to get them to the site any way, don't you?" she'd said.

Dave hadn't even looked up from the paper, as though the need to move was so obvious to him. Now Robin wondered if he'd been hiding, because he'd had no answers for some of the arguments she might have advanced.

"Yes, that's true," he'd said. "But my clients seem to think North Dakota is the back of beyond. It'll be easier from Minneapolis. I'll make all the arrangements to get to the site from there."

"Is that where you're moving to, Minneapolis?" Of course she hadn't really questioned him or objected. His announcement had frightened her badly, although she'd tried not to let that show. Was he leaving her and Sunny?

Reconsidering that morning, Robin realized that Dave hadn't been casual at all.

He'd said, "It's not *I'm* moving. *We're* moving, right? Wouldn't you like to live there? They say it's a terrific city, with wonderful schools. I bet the school system here isn't much."

"Well, Sunny's just three. I guess I hadn't thought about it too much. I'm sure Minneapolis is a lovely place."

"We'll go in early next week and look at houses," Dave said, as though the idea of moving to the Twin Cities had been discussed for months, instead of being raised for the first time over a morning cup of coffee on a stormy April day. And, she loved the idea of buying a house instead of renting.

There had been a series of hate crimes in Fargo about that time, all aimed at the tiny Jewish community. Tombstones had been toppled in their cemetery. The only synagogue in town had been spray-painted with obscenities. Several Jewish citizens of Fargo, including a star high school athlete, had received packets of hate mail accusing Jews of horrible crimes.

Could that have been what triggered Dave's need to move? It seemed so unlikely. But Dave's annex was highly unlikely and it certainly existed.

In Fargo, Robin had been appalled by the vandalism. "Look at this story," she'd said, rattling her newspaper for emphasis. "Why would anyone need to do this? Desecrate a Jewish synagogue and cemetery. Awful."

Dave had looked over her shoulder. "It says Hitler's birthday is in April. These neo-Nazis do it as a memorial to him." Dave's hand had come down across Robin's shoulder, fast and hard, his finger poking at the column of type further down in the story. His actions were fierce, almost forcing the paper out her hands.

"See. The Anti-Defamation League is in town to look it over. There's a community meeting, too."

His finger had stabbed at the notice of the meeting: once, twice, three times.

Robin had looked up. Dave's actions were usually so controlled. But he had moved away. He'd already left the kitchen for the office he'd set up in their spare bedroom.

"Are you going to the meeting?" she'd called after him.

His voice had floated back to her. "There's nothing you can do to change something like that," he'd said before shutting the door between them.

Dave put down the phone after speaking to Robin. She didn't have the flu. This was going to be just as bad as he'd feared. He hadn't even been able to bring up the subject of her meetings with Jess and the others. She hadn't mentioned it either, or referred in any way to what they'd told her. What if she didn't come back? Oh, she'd be back for Sunny; that was certain. She'd be back to arrange for his care. Robin was one of the most responsible people in the world, responsible enough to look after his child, his money, his precious assets, if she had to.

Too bad they'd cut him out of his heavy cast that morning. He could have pounded on that without doing any harm. His new brace didn't offer the same kind of barrier, or protection.

Just then he'd practically have given his life to be able to walk up the two flights of stairs to his office, to lock the door, then open his bookcase doorway and walk down the stairs into his annex, picking out a book as he went. His fingers flexed as though he could actually feel the binding. He could almost smell the sharp scent of fresh-cut lumber that lingered there; the fragrance of safety to him. But was it? Or, had he somehow confused activity with anxiety, using one to temper the other?

When he'd first thought of moving he'd never considered building an annex. His only thought had been to get away from the anti-Semitic attacks in Fargo.

Then, when their Realtor showed them the house they'd finally bought, the most worn of the three houses they'd seen that day, she'd said, "This was originally a farmhouse, one of the first in the area. Look at how they built things then."

Her gesture had swept around the low-ceilinged third floor, unfinished boards and dust. "This is no trap door attic like you'll find in many of houses of this era. You've got a real third floor here. You get a lot more space for your money. Of course, there's no second set of stairs, servant's stairs. Most farmhouses didn't have them. But, then, who needs them today?"

Dave was going to shoot back some clever answering comment about servants, but at that moment he looked down the short staircase they had just ascended. That was all he should have been able to see. Instead, for a few seconds it was as if the house had become transparent. A strikingly clear view of all the levels of the house appeared before him. Dave also saw a whole new structure in place, a staircase-bunker, superimposed on his momentary X-ray view of the house.

That was the moment when the old farmhouse became a haven to Dave.

Standing in the attic that day, Dave had been so surprised by what he'd just seen that he'd almost spoken his plan out loud. "There's room for… "

He'd stopped. Suddenly he had a new and crucial secret to hold close, a secret that would insure safety.

He could even have his parents stay with them if real danger threatened. They would all be safe.

So, he hadn't said a word. They had left the attic and gone downstairs. By the time they'd reached the first floor, Dave had formulated his plans to modify the bedrooms. He had selected an exit, figured out how to handle air circulation, plumbing, and lighting. It seemed to him that he had been mandated to build the annex. He'd just been handed a simple equation: if he did the work he could stay with Robin and Sunny forever.

The stairwell would have to be secret. Secrets were a part of every bargain that had anything to do with survival. Dave's true identity had to be a secret; so why not the annex?

Lying in his hospital bed he knew he could ring the bell and one of the orderlies or nurses would come and say, "What can I do for you, Dave?"

He'd have no answer. No one could help.

He reached back, pounding his fist into the pile of pillows behind his head. He only succeeded in tearing apart the neat arrangement the nurse had set up for him.

It hadn't been as comfortable as when Robin did it, anyway.

CHAPTER TWENTY-FOUR

Around five-thirty on Wednesday afternoon Wolff walked slowly toward the front door of the hospital, on his way home. He should have been dancing for joy, but he walked like a man with a great burden.

Just that morning he'd flown his last delivery trip ever, supplies for the High Holy Days, even prayer books for the services that several small communities had planned with his help.

He was finished forever with needing multiple jobs to keep his family fed. He was finished with the physical labor and stress of the meat packing plant.

The *Rav* and Faiga's father had finally invited them back to the East Coast to run a retreat center located in New Jersey, just across the river from Faiga's family.

It was the perfect job. Faiga would handle bookings and he would create the programs. The retreat center would be in a mansion, part of an estate that had been donated to their group. The four-bedroom, three-bath estate manager's house would be their new home.

So, why wasn't he dancing with happiness and triumph? Was he the only member of his family who would miss living in South Dakota?

In New Jersey his children would have the most wonderful schools to attend, and he would be able to study, too. Now he could finally become a real rabbi.

"Rabbi, Rabbi Blumen.

"CHAPLAIN BLUMEN!"

The voice of the hospital's receptionist had fit so seamless into his reverie it had taken her loud reminder of his present job to break through. "You're behaving as though you've left us already," the woman said, mock reproach in her voice. "But we haven't let you go yet." She'd been at the front desk all his years in Sioux Falls, so they were old friends.

"There's someone waiting for you in the chapel," she said.

Wolff turned and trudged back in that direction. Maybe it was Al Logan. He kept hoping the newsman would show up, since he would have to talk to him about following Robin to Minneapolis. That was one of the things holding him in Sioux Falls. It wasn't just nostalgia. He also felt a profound sense of responsibility to Dave, Sunny, and Robin, and to Al Logan. That complex of relationships had to be resolved before he could go anywhere.

His visitor was an elderly man, sitting quietly in one of the chapel pews, hiding his nervousness except for the restless handling of his fedora, which he turned around and around in his hands. Like the hat, all his clothing was formal, a suit, white shirt, tie, and topcoat.

Wolff had only taken a few steps into the chapel when the man stood up and advanced toward him.

There certainly was something familiar about him. Even before he spoke Wolff knew he would have an accent.

"I'm…." Wolff began.

"Wolff Blumen. You are the man I must thank. You are the man who saved my son's life."

Of course, this man was Dave's father.

"Mr. Razkowski…"

"Please, you will call me Jacob. Better that I not use my last name here. But, on behalf of my whole family, we all thank you."

"How did you find us, find Dave?" Wolff asked as he invited Jacob Razkowski into the nearby chaplain's office.

When they were seated, he reached for the phone, never letting his eyes leave the older man's face. He called home. "Faiga, I'll be a little late, maybe a half hour. There's a situation here…I have a visitor…"

"And you might need to bring the situation home for dinner," Faiga guessed.

"Right," Wolff said.

He hung up the phone. He and his visitor were looking straight into each other's eyes. The office was so small their knees almost touched. No wonder this man had looked so familiar. He was an aged version of his son, with the same thin face, the same intense look in his grey eyes. He even had the same full head of hair, except that his was snow white.

"So, Rabbi, you asked how I found you. It is a marvelous age. My older son finds the list of all the hospitals in South Dakota for me, and I phone them. That is how I find David. You, the hospital tells me about. So you are the ideal place to start."

"You'll want to see Dave first thing, of course," said Wolff, half rising.

"No. That I cannot do. If others see me with my David, then they will know he is Jewish. I cannot hide myself as he does. My wife and I, the whole family, we are my David's big secret. Only I must know how he is. So, once I find the hospital, of course I must come here."

"You came all the way to Sioux Falls, and you don't expect to see Dave?"

"I came from Detroit. I must know more than a phone call will tell me. I must know that David is not unconscious, not dying, God forbid. When I try to call his house – I never call his house, always he calls me – but when I do not hear from him for such a long time, I risk it. No one answers no matter when I phone. So, it means Robin is not there, no one is there. For a while I think I will call his neighbor, the rabbi and her husband who live next door. Fortunately I know the name. But once I find the hospital, first I must fly here and make sure my David is not ..."

He stopped. No matter how controlled Jacob Razkowski seemed to be, the thought that his son might have died clearly overwhelmed him.

Wolff leaned back in his desk chair. "Mr. Razkowski, I can tell you absolutely that David is mending. He's not well yet. There will have to be a lot of physical therapy. He will be all right though, probably one hundred percent all right."

Jacob Razkowski leaned forward, as though following Wolff. "So, I should ask the doctor to make him less all right, less then one hundred percent. They should leave him with enough problems to keep him on the ground, away from mountain climbing all alone and other foolishness. If he goes again, one day he will be killed."

Jacob Razkowski had obviously anticipated this accident for years. Dave might never see his father, but clearly they were in touch. Jacob knew where Dave lived. He knew about his family. He even knew about his neighbors.

Mrs. Raz...," Wolff began, but the old man interrupted again.

"Please, it must only be Jacob here, unless my son will say otherwise, which he will never do."

Wolff stood up. "If you cannot see Dave, then you must come home with me for dinner. Dave's...Sunny, your granddaughter, is staying with us right now. Can you meet her without ...?"

Jacob didn't need to hear more. He stood up too, but slowly. Wolff wanted to offer the older man his arm, but he felt that it would be rejected. Did Dave have any idea how frail his father seemed to be?

"So, Rabbi, as I said, we will use no last names. Not at your house either. Sunny only needs to know that my name is Jacob. To meet her will be a gift. And her mother, Robin, will be there too?"

"Robin is in Minneapolis right now, although we expect her back soon."

"Then before she comes, we will make a strategy. Maybe she will approve. Finally I will speak to her, no matter what David wants. We must stop this from happening again."

It took only a minute to brief Faiga before Wolff introduced Jacob to all the children. It wasn't difficult to pick Sunny out of the crowd. He sat Jacob beside her, praying that proximity wasn't too much for the old man.

However fragile Jacob Razkowski might be physically, his emotional toughness remained evident. He paid almost equal attention to all the children. Only Wolff could see that his eyes rested on Sunny as she ate, then followed her after dinner as she helped Faiga and Shayna clear the table while the boys pushed in chairs and ran the vacuum cleaner.

CHAPTER TWENTY-FIVE

Al left Minneapolis very late on Wednesday. He had his whole return trip planned down to the minute.

He would arrive in the middle of the night so that he could get into the KLON studio during the three hours of the day the building was closed, 2 a.m. to 5 a.m.

When he had what he wanted he'd leave, returning to broadcast the morning news as though he'd just arrived back in town. In the afternoon he'd make one run to his apartment. He'd take whatever was back from the dry cleaners, his freshly laundered shirts, his best sweaters, whatever fit in his two suitcases. The cleaning crew could have the rest. He'd store his secret library in the trunk of his rented car until he bought himself a car later in the day. Then he'd check into a Sioux Falls hotel for one week at the most.

All the way back to Sioux Falls his mother's voice had filled his ears, all her old stories about leaving Hungary. This time he welcomed her voice because he knew it would never again repeat, "They're coming."

After the realization in Dave's annex, he'd never see her again anyway. He couldn't. But that didn't mean he'd lose what he'd learned from her. She would always be the embodiment of survival to him.

She had to have been the spirit behind the whole family when all of them–his mother, father and grand-mother–had decided that taking the risk of leaving Communist Hungary was worthwhile. She'd always been the one to tell the story. "It was the only thing for us to do," she'd always said. That made perfect sense to Al now. *White Hot* was the only thing for him to do.

He'd just been through two days of ceaseless effort, and it hadn't felt like work for one moment.

My god, now he was even quoting his father. When one of his children tried to get him to slow down, Anatoly Lowenthal always said, "This is not work. This is mine. That makes it my pleasure."

Of course. *White Hot* was his. And, he didn't have to do it alone, because he had a secret helper, his alter-ego, Alton Lowenthal.

Shortly after two a.m., right on schedule, Al let himself into the studio and went straight to what the staff called the catastrophe files: floods, hurricanes, earthquakes, and Holocaust footage.

He'd written his screenplay in the first few hours after he'd raced down the stairs of Dave's bunker—he loved that Robin had tried to catch him, it hadn't even frightened him. He'd hired his main actors later that day, a tall thin man with long brown hair and a pretty blonde woman. Robin was very pretty. The talent agency was finding a little girl for his show. Maybe he'd add a boy who could learn carpentry from his father. That would be a great touch. Al had looked into his rear view mirror at that, grinning at his reflection. He could do real life better than the actual people.

For once his agent in Chicago was earning his money. He'd been excited right from the first moment.

White Hot was half sold during their first conversation. "Just give me the proposal," his agent said. "The cable channels are crazy for this kind of stuff. *White Hot!* You're even giving them a great title."

Dave's annex would be the pilot for *White Hot*. That's why Al needed the Holocaust footage from the station's files. They'd never miss it, but if they did, they'd just assume that some intern or clerk had misfiled it. He took all the footage of the White Supremacist enclaves in the area. He could get it other ways, but that would take time, and might give away one or more of his ideas. He took every scrap of coverage of Dave's accident. Who knew what he could get away with showing?

By the weekend he'd have a contract for a TV series, once a month on cable. He'd fly to Atlanta to sign the papers. It was the new year, *Rosh Hashanah*. What better time to start a new life? *White Hot* would be the TV sensation of the decade. Al's plan was to tell stories so intense, so intimate, that the real people involved had to be spared the pain of actually appearing on television. Instead they'd let a sensitive journalist–that was Al–dramatize their story.

Standing in the darkened building and going through the disaster files felt like part of a great victory. Just standing there, another whole range of ideas occurred to him. He took material on Jewish holidays too, the High Holy

Days, kids lighting Chanukah candles. Wolff Blumen's life would be good for several shows.

Wolff had been unwilling to leave him alone since the night he'd tricked him into telling his family's story. At their second meeting, in the miniscule Chaplain's office at the hospital, Al had been stunned to find out that Wolff had once been William Flowers.

He hadn't thought of *White Hot* at that time of course, but he'd had to protest Wolff's giving up a show business career. "I actually saw you perform in a club on a visit to New York," he'd told Wolff. "You were good; funny, and dirty too. I guess you'd have called it bawdy. That was you, my god."

"Right," Wolff agreed. "My God; that used to be me."

"Used to be?" Al asked. "How can you just say it like that? You had a following, you could have been big."

At least Wolff hadn't laughed. He didn't say how much better his life was now. How could he? He hadn't said that Al ought to try it. He'd just said, "It was good in its own way, but too expensive for me in the long run. I had to stop."

"So you gave up show business and joined a cult," Al had said, deliberately trying to provoke Blumen. He couldn't believe that this man was a loony Moonie.

But Wolff just responded in that quiet voice, "It's not a cult. In a cult I probably wouldn't have any more pain, the same kind of pain you have. You can't understand your parents, really. You want to love them, protect them against anything and everything. And then again, almost at the same time, you're furious because your life has been so different from what's supposed to be normal."

Al could see the anguish in Wolff's face as he spoke.

"I used to tell myself it was different because they were immigrants. Or because they were Polish Jews and everyone else we knew was a Russian or German Jew.

"They were older than other parents, lots older. I spent years ascribing every difference to that. And I was an only child. That was another big thing."

Even Wolff hadn't made complete peace with his dead parents' history. So why should Al expect peace? He could operate without it.

"All those things, and I would never touch the basic difference. My parents had been to hell and back, and that's a trip that changes you forever. They had nightmares. They had rages. They were terrified of ordinary things. A policeman on a street corner nearby could panic them. And then in the stories they told so matter-of-factly, they were so brave. I couldn't believe anyone could be that brave. I couldn't. I wasn't even supposed to be afraid when they talked about dying.

"I used to wonder how come they knew things no one else knew. They knew the Nazis would be back. No one else did.

"And I couldn't imagine how I could ever be like them, which is a problem because you're supposed to be like your parents. But how could you ever get to be like two people who'd lost their whole family, their children? It was an impassable gulf. I couldn't understand how to navigate it. I still can't."

He had smiled then, but Al could only see sadness. When Al got to his version of Wolff's stories he would make him sadder than the clowns in the circus with permanent down-turned mouths and forever-tears painted on their faces.

"You are the same," Wolff had said to Al.

Al vowed that no one would ever say things like that to him again. It was too much like receiving a horrible medical prognosis, or hearing your own obituary.

But, he would get at least two great editions of *White Hot* out the time he'd spent with Wolff. One would focus on religious conversions and epiphanies, another would examine why people gave up fame for obscurity.

CHAPTER TWENTY-SIX

When the door bell rang after dinner, Faiga was swept by a momentary sense of *déjà vu*. She dismissed it as she went to the door. She wouldn't have to deal with Al Logan. Wolff had answered the door that night.

Robin stood on the front stoop with her backpack on one shoulder and her jacket over her arm.

This was a Robin Faiga had never seen before, pale and hollow-eyed. She had never thought it possible for Robin to look plain.

As she stood aside to let Robin in, Faiga glanced over her shoulder to where the two men, Jacob and Wolff, sat in the living room.

"I'm beat," Robin said. She put her hand on Faiga's arm in greeting. "If you'll call Sunny I'll be on my way. It's only eight, so I didn't think they'd be in bed already."

"No," Faiga said, "They're still playing upstairs, but they're probably in pajamas already." She didn't want Sunny downstairs just then.

Wolff had obviously seen and heard Robin come in, because suddenly he was standing beside Faiga. Across the room Jacob had risen politely.

Then several things happened at once. Sunny came bounding down the stairs to share the delicious fun of wearing one of Shayna's nightgowns, while her friend was dressed in her pajamas. Jacob crossed the room toward the group at the door. Faiga moved toward the old man to warn him against surprising Robin, especially with Sunny right there. In the same instant she realized that Jacob understood everything he saw, Faiga heard a muffled exclamation from Wolff and Sunny's cry, "Mommy, Mommy."

Faiga put out her hand toward Jacob: to stop him, to support him? Jacob had reached toward her too, likely for the same reasons. As she turned back toward the front door – how could she be so far way from her friend in such a short time and in such a small house – she saw that Wolff had caught Robin as she'd slumped to the floor.

"Mommy, Mommy." Sunny was frantically pulling at Robin. Wolff's right arm was tight around Robin's shoulders.

By then Faiga had reached the little girl. "She's okay, Sunny, honestly. She probably felt faint, just a tiny little bit faint. Wolff caught her. She'll be okay. She drove most of the day to get here and probably forgot to eat. She wanted to see you and your Daddy so badly. You have to give her a minute, that's all."

But Sunny kept right on crying hysterically, "Mommy, Mommy," and looking around the room desperately, as though to find whatever had caused her mother's collapse. Jacob hovered nearby. Clearly he wanted to sweep the little girl up in his arms to comfort her, but didn't dare. Sunny looked up into Jacob's grey eyes, her own so similar. Accusingly, she said, "You scared her. You look a lot like my Daddy you know, 'cept lots older. That scared her."

Later Faiga would have time to be amazed by how calmly Jacob Razkowski handled Sunny's outburst.

"Then your Daddy must be a very handsome fellow," he said. Faiga heard Wolff laugh and Robin's weak voice say, "Sunny, I'm okay. I'm just really tired. Faiga is right. She's going to give me something to eat. You and Shayna please go upstairs."

Faiga went out to the kitchen for a glass of water. When she returned Sunny still hovered over her mother who now sat on the small sofa under the front window. Shayna was standing on the bottom stair, unwilling to leave Sunny. Wolff, who normally wouldn't even shake hands with a woman, was checking Robin's pulse.

When Wolff saw her return to the living room, he released Robin's hand gently and stood up. Faiga read his message: Robin was okay and it was more appropriate for Faiga to minister to her. She sat down beside Robin. Wolff, obviously fearful that he might have a second patient this evening, had moved over to where Jacob sat at the dinning room table.

It took several minutes after that, but finally the adults agreed that Sunny would spend one more night at the Blumens. The two little girls were then hustled off to bed, still in each other's night wear, with promises of two bedtime stories the next night. Faiga had made Robin a sandwich, poured her a glass of lemonade, and watched her eat and drink while Wolff sat with Jacob, the two talking quietly

Oddly, it was Jacob who finally took the initiative. "Sunny said I frightened you. Out of the mouth of babes, you would say. I apologize for appearing without warning. I didn't realize that I look so much like... I certainly never meant to.... I just wanted to make sure..."

Although Robin was still pale she sat up straight and tried to smile at Jacob.

"You do look very much alike. And, please don't apologize. Despite what Sunny said you didn't frighten me. It was just that seeing you, on top of everything else that's happened..."

"We're not going to get much done here if no one ever manages to finish a sentence," Wolff said. "Robin, you must have a lot to tell us if Jacob isn't the biggest surprise you've had lately."

No one had mentioned Dave by name yet, but he was so much on everyone's mind he might just as well have been right there.

CHAPTER TWENTY-SEVEN

Facing Dave couldn't be any harder than all the things she'd dealt with in the last few days, Robin told herself on the way to the hospital the morning after she returned to Sioux Falls. So many secrets, right down to why he'd selected Sunny's proper names, Sarah and Elizabeth.

But, even with everything Dave had done, she felt as though the four of them had done so much plotting against him. Could more secrets be right, even if they were for Dave's own good?

It was a relief to be alone. She'd insisted that Jacob sleep in this morning. When they'd said good night he'd insisted that he would get up and take her to breakfast, to be there, unseen, when she confronted Dave. But Robin had insisted that he rest. By the end of the evening at the Blumen's, Robin thought Jacob looked as though he might faint too.

It had taken every ounce of determination to tell Wolff, Faiga and Jacob about Dave's annex. How she'd wished she could comfort Jacob as she'd spoken. He had sat, his neck bowed, like a beast with too heavy a load to pull. In the end she had stopped before telling them anything at all about Al Logan's visits to her home.

"I don't know what to talk to Dave about first," she'd admitted. "There's the fact that he has more money, more property, assets, than he ever told me about. Of course that really is his business."

She'd looked around the room. No one agreed with her.

"Not that he should have done that, not told me," Robin said. "But compared to the annex, it doesn't seem so bad. After all, it's only money."

She turned to Jacob. "Dave has files about you; your whole life story and your wife's, too. I saw all the documents from Poland, reparations from Germany, everything, all translated, plus a memoir, pages and pages of it."

"Testimony," Jacob said. "There are groups that collect the stories of survivors. David wrote to me and his mother about it. I thought if we did that, maybe he would come home. It seemed…it was not so hard to do, really."

"But he didn't come," Robin said.

"No, he did not," Jacob said, the admission obviously paining him. "He could not. He kept saying, next week, next month, after the next job. I knew he could not do it. Finally I had the testimony sent to him. By then I knew he would keep it, read it over and over. I had not realized that it could make things worse, not better. I never should have done it. I should not have told him anything at all. I should have said nothing. All this is my fault. I suppose I needed to hear it one more time, for it to be important to one more person that I love."

"You had to tell him," Wolff protested. "It's his right to know. You're right to tell your story."

But Jacob was adamant. "No, his nature was different from my other children. What had happened was so much farther away from David's life. I should have said nothing. Some he would have learned, anyway. His brother and sister could have told him a little. When I talked about it I frightened him. Or, perhaps it revolted him. We never mention it. I am his father—his mother does not tell her story, except in testimony she was willing. But I am his father; I should have understood his nature."

Robin and Jacob had ended up sitting next to each other on the Blumen's sofa. As Jacob spoke Robin had reached over to pat his hand. When she struggled to tell them about the annex Jacob had taken her hand in his. The gesture was so touching that Robin had started to cry. That set Faiga off. "I'm sorry." Faiga said through her tears, "I can see how hard this is, and I can't think of any way to help either one of you."

"Faiga has done her share on this kind of rehabilitation with me," Wolff explained. "You should have seen her face the first time I told her my parents thought my being a child actor was the safest way to live. So we could playact, and then always be on the move when the Nazis came back. I've never seen anyone so shocked."

"How could you not tell Dave your story?" Wolff had demanded of Jacob. "It's his right to know. How could you have kept it a secret anyway? It's part of you. It's always with you. Think about it. The only question you've asked me since we met that hasn't been directly about Dave, was if you could attend *Yizkor* services with us this weekend."

Wolff turned to Robin. "*Yizkor* is a memorial service held during most major Jewish holidays. Jacob will attend services with us this weekend, for *Rosh Hashanah.*"

"I'll go with you," Robin said to Jacob without even thinking about it.

Jacob patted her hand again. "It's an Orthodox service," he explained. "You'll have to sit up above or to one side and watch. You won't understand a word."

"I'll sit with Faiga and she'll explain," Robin said, looking over at her friend who nodded agreement. "If that's what you want, Robin," Faiga said.

The old man could not go alone. How could David neglect his father this way? Even though Robin now knew that Dave sent gifts, a check every month, pictures of her and Sunny, he didn't go himself. That was neglect.

But, the next morning, despite how she felt about what Dave had done to his father, despite what she'd found at home, despite her resolve as she drove to the hospital, she greeted Dave as though nothing unusual had happened. She kissed him. His breakfast tray was there so she raised the end of his bed, arranged his pillows for him so he could eat comfortably, then she said, "Oh, you're going to need a clean gown and towels." Then she fled the room leaving Dave balancing a spoonful of oatmeal in his left hand and looking very surprised.

Twice during the day she phoned Jacob, waiting for her at the small hospital apartment that Wolff had arranged for him.

For the first time in weeks she also called Faiga during the day, supposedly to check on Sunny. The second time she called Faiga said to her, "Robin, you don't have to do this alone. You don't have to do it at all. You don't have to confront Dave, if you don't want to. We all know how hard it is. Wolff will come with you, or Jacob. Or, you can wait until Dave's mother arrives. She's staying in Detroit for the holidays, to be with her son and daughter and their families, but she'll be here late Sunday night. I spoke to her briefly. She sounds just as nice as Jacob. She says 'my David,' just like he does."

But Robin knew she couldn't wait. They didn't even know the full breadth of things that she had to say to Dave. How could she be such a coward? Who knew what Al Logan would do with what he'd discovered in their home?

In fact, Dave was the one who confronted her the third time she returned to his room.

"You seem to be avoiding me," he said.

If he's willing to challenge me, he thinks he might be home free, Robin told herself. She found strength in that idea. He's a little confused, but he's betting that he's still in control. He's wondering if we can possibly go on just like before. He probably thinks I want that too, so I won't react.

What she really wanted to do was put her hands on Dave's shoulders, never mind his injuries, and shake him. She wanted to yell at him, "You idiot. Your father is here, worried sick, and you've never even mentioned him, much less that he's a good and decent person who worries about you all the time."

"Why do you say that?" she said to Dave. "Because I'm not here hovering over you every single minute? You're out of that heavy cast now; you can manage occasionally on your own."

It was hard to know who was more surprised by what she'd just said. Robin had trouble believing those words had just come out of her mouth. Dave looked as though she'd struck him.

"The dietician," he sputtered. "You've never worried about what they've been feeding me, and now you go and spend an hour with the dietician?"

Robin had no clear idea of what she was going to say. She couldn't remember a single word she'd rehearsed.

But something fundamental in her life had shifted and it was up to her to let Dave know that. All she could do was straighten up … as though she were teaching a class. She could breathe properly, inhaling deeply. She could hold her spine perfectly straight. Then, speaking so slowly she could almost see the words form as they came out of her mouth she finally said, "You probably wonder why I haven't mentioned any of the things that Jess Lansdowne and the others told me?"

The smile on Dave's face faded completely. His expression went blank. She'd seen him do that before she realized; transform his face into a neutral mask whenever she'd touched on things he didn't want to discuss. How could it have taken her so many years to recognize that?

Dave drew in a deep breath too, like a man about to dive into a deep pool. "Well, yes. But with you ducking in and out of the room all day it's been hard to bring up the subject."

If he'd said that before the trip to Minneapolis it would have crushed her. "You would never have brought it up," she said flatly.

"Then why would I have sent you to Minneapolis?" he countered.

"Because you had no choice," Robin said. "But the money, the house, that's only one piece of it, and not the most important piece."

Dave raised one eyebrow; as if to say he could hardly believe that the house and money weren't important to her.

That raised eyebrow was like a red flag.

"David Eli Razkowski, I want you to listen to me," Robin said.

With his full name hovering in the air between them like a living thing, Dave froze. His jaw locked, a vein in his forehead suddenly pulsed.

"David…" Robin started again.

"David! David Eli! Where did you hear that? Why are you suddenly calling me David?"

"Well it's your name, isn't it? Dave, David, what's the difference?"

"There's a big difference. You've never called me David before. I make sure no one ever calls me 'David,' no one. And how do you even know that Eli is my middle name? I never told you that! Where did you ever hear that? Have you been…have you been talking to someone, to my family? How did you get to them? No one ever calls me that. It's Dave. David is too…"

"Is too much like what your father calls you?" Robin flung the words back at him. "In fact, I happen to know it's exactly what your father calls you. Does it remind you too much of your old home and your family, and you can't handle that? Or, is it that deep down Sunny and I really embarrass you too much for us to actually meet them?"

It seemed impossible that she could become so angry so quickly. She must have had this stored away deep inside for a very long time.

"Or, is it just too Jewish? Honest, Dave, not to tell me you're Jewish. Did you think I wouldn't love you? How could you believe that of me?

"David, your name is David. It's a lovely, strong name. What's wrong with the name your parents gave you? What's wrong with both your names? It's like Sunny's names. I mean her real names from the Bible, Sa'arah Elisheva, not Sarah Elizabeth."

Robin had paused a second or two, to make sure she got the exotic Hebrew pronunciation absolutely correct, but she'd held up one hand to Dave at the same time, to keep him silent.

She went on, "Although you've made sure no one ever calls her by those names, English or Hebrew. You came up with Sunny, too. Not that you've ever told me who she was really named for, or why."

All the fight had suddenly drained out of Dave, along with the normal color in his face. Under the remnants of his faded tan he was sickly pale.

"How do you...do you know all this?"

Robin plowed on. "How could you do that? As if you own a piece of Sunny exclusively. As if you think there's some big part of her that has nothing to do with me. Did you think I wouldn't want her named for your grandmothers?"

The secrets that had to do with Sunny hurt worst of all, so there was a little catch in Robin's voice when she said, "I love that she's connected to family that way. Of course their history, that's awful. But, she should know that eventually. I should have known already, that there is something in her name that big, that important. But, no matter what, you can't own a part of her – by yourself, I mean. She's as much my daughter as yours. In fact, maybe she's more mine, because we're not married. Whatever her first name is, her last name is McDonald, not Razkowski."

It didn't seem possible, but Dave looked even more shocked that he had just seconds before, and a little lost. "You can't mean that. Neither one of us has more of Sunny than the other," he protested. "And, you never actually said you wanted to be married."

"Of course I've never said. You made it clear that you didn't want to get married. I didn't want to … I couldn't tell you that we ought to be married. I wanted to be asked, properly asked. And I wasn't exactly in a position to debate the point when I was pregnant."

"Did I ever say I wouldn't marry you?"

"Did you ever say you would? Did you ever ask? Not that I would necessarily, not now."

"You mean because I'm lying here in bed, crippled?"

If Robin had been angry before, now a level of temper flared that she'd never thought she could posses. She walked right up to head of Dave's bed, bent down, and glared at him.

"How dare you!" she said, her face only inches from his. "How dare you use the accident that you caused yourself, to attack me? Your crazy yearly trip and the risks you took for some obscure psychological reason that you can't or won't explain to anyone. This isn't the moment to discuss marriage, that's all I meant. How dare you even suggest that I would desert you, or anyone, under these circumstances?"

Apparently this is what it took to break through to Dave. She had to turn his world upside down. His stunned look told her that he'd never seen her really angry before, never heard her raise her voice.

"Robin, listen. I didn't mean…" Dave tried to reach for her from his position in bed, but she backed away.

"I don't want to know what you mean. Right now we're talking about what we do, not what we mean. Listen! Your father went looking for you when you didn't phone as usual. He checked every single hospital in the state. At least he knew you were in South Dakota. Otherwise, he'd have checked the whole country."

Just thinking about Jacob's suffering made her angrier. How could Dave do that to his own father, a man who'd always supported and love him? Her own father was so long gone she couldn't even remember him.

"Your father, a lovely man – the one who calls you David – worries about you all the time. But he especially worries about this yearly trip, just as I do. And he knows all about Sunny and me, although I knew nothing about him or the rest of your family."

Dave couldn't have broken in now if he'd wanted to. There was no interrupting her. She wasn't even looking at him any more. She was pacing up and down in the space beside the bed, like a lawyer summing up a case in court.

"That's another thing," she said. "You told him about us. You sent pictures to your family. But you never told me. It's like you owned us, as if we were animals in your private zoo. How could you?"

The fact that Dave had done things that deprived Sunny of family hurt more than anything else.

"Your parents are the only grandparents our daughter is ever likely to know. I don't even know where my mother is these days. And Sunny has cousins, aunts and uncles, but you've kept her from them. They're the only outside family she's ever likely to know."

She had stopped pacing. She looked across the small room at Dave who was clearly trying to gather up the energy to say something. He'd raised his left hand, pointing his index finger at her.

She knew the next things she had to say would stop him cold. It felt like a low blow, but she had to go on.

"And, Dave, there's your annex! No, don't interrupt. It's my turn. I know, I know you must have been…badly frightened, I guess…to do that, to build that thing into our house, to put it there, above us, behind the wall in our bedroom, without telling me.

Then she did have to stop for a moment. She heard the sob in her own voice. She wasn't going to show any weakness. But, it had to be said. The annex had frightened her so, had made Dave a stranger. "I don't know if I'll ever be able to understand that, ever be able to… to be with you again, and not think about it. All the things you said you built into the house for me, and they weren't for me at all. I recognize you likely thought it was for all of us, for our safety, if some awful nightmare of yours should ever come true. But you can't decide those things for me."

"How did you find it? How do you know about that?"

By now Robin's agitation was just as extreme as Dave's. Her face had flushed as Dave had blanched white. She locked her fingers into tight fists to stop her hands from shaking. She set her jaw. She had to get through this part, no matter how hard it was for her, no matter how hard it was on Dave.

She had just thrown a laundry list of issues and complaints at a man who couldn't fight back. Surely, she'd taken unfair advantage. But she couldn't think about that now. She raised her chin and stood up straight. It had never been harder to do. Somehow she kept her voice steady.

"It all happened at once. I found your stairway, your annex. I know all about it. I got all sorts of new information on the trip home. I got the messages you sent through Jess and Company, and I understood. They explained everything to me. I know that the way you've set up the deed, it's at least partly my house. I suppose I should thank you for that. But, you know what? Before anyone says thank you for anything, we have to decide what it all means."

She spoke almost conversationally now that Dave had stopped trying to interrupt. The news about his annex had taken the fight out of him. He seemed to have burrowed deeper into the bed.

Robin continued, "You can't run away, even if you want to. But, then, I can't run away either. I've got to stay right here and see you through this. I want to. I don't much care whether you want me to or not. You can't fight me. That makes it easier. I'm your physical therapist and your lifeline for at least the next few months. And you're my income and Sunny's security. I suppose that's one reason it's not really a level playing field, that you still have something of an advantage. But, at least I have some advantages for the moment. That will have to do for now."

Finally she turned her back on Dave, moving toward the door.

"I'll be back tomorrow, but not until the afternoon. You don't have to worry about your father. He never expected to see you. He wouldn't do anything that might embarrass or upset you. The way you choose to do things is okay with him. It's not okay with me. You don't have to worry about Sunny either. She doesn't know who he is, except a nice man named Jacob who can peel apples with a knife and remember all the names of her stuffed animals after only one introduction."

She had her hand on the door knob now. She had finally slumped, her extra-straight posture forgotten. Her voice was barely audible. Dave seemed to understand that she was saying much of this for herself, even though the words were addressed to him.

"I'm going," she said. "If you think of anything you want to say, if you have questions, write them down."

Once outside she sagged back against the nearest wall. She had done it. But she hadn't completed the job. She hadn't told Dave anything about Al Logan. How would she ever find the nerve to talk about that?

CHAPTER TWENTY-EIGHT

It wouldn't be until after the weekend that the next phase of the plan Wolff, Faiga, Jacob and Robin had agreed to could be put in place.

The delay made for a couple of very hard days. Robin had to keep Sunny away from Dave so she wouldn't chatter on about Jacob and Margarita. It was better if Dave thought his father had come and gone without seeing him. Of course Sunny's absence immediately made Dave suspicious. "She has a cold," Robin said briefly, "That's the last thing you need."

On both Saturday and Sunday morning she'd gone to the Blumen's house and walked with Faiga to a tiny house that served as a synagogue for the few orthodox families in Sioux Falls.

Jacob was right, she didn't understand a word. But Faiga had brought her a prayer book with English translations, and a book about the High Holy Days, *Rosh Hashanah* and *Yom Kippur.* Faiga had told Robin she could ignore the rest of the congregation when they

245

stood. Was it like kneeling in a Catholic church, Robin wanted to know? To show respect for God, to get closer to Him, Faiga whispered to her. After that Robin stood with the rest of the congregation.

All the women at the service sat together, apart from the men, behind a flimsy screen and over to one side of the tiny sanctuary. Through the wide gaps in the screen Robin could see Jacob occasionally adjusting the huge white and black striped prayer shawl he wore. He stood beside Wolff as though in a protective shadow. "It's a gift for Wolff that Jacob is here," Faiga said. "Nothing is ever all bad. Wolff never got to attend *shul* with his own father."

Then at lunch Wolff did some thing that turned out to be another shock for Robin in what had been weeks of shocks. The children had eaten and gone to play when he said, "It is traditional to learn a little at the Sabbath table and during the holidays. Plus, the new year is the time to correct things, between people and between ourselves and God. I have something to correct."

Robin could see that Faiga looked concerned, but not surprised. Obviously she knew what Wolff was about to do.

"Usually we learn from the Five Books of Moses, the *Torah*. But, today we have to talk about things much more recent, but almost as important. The most recent chapter of these events began when I spotted Dave. It was as though God…" Wolff gestured toward the sky, "…as though God intended to bring us all together."

Beside her Robin heard Jacob make a small, almost hostile sound that seemed to discount God's involvement, at least in his life.

"Robin," Wolff said, "You should know that when Al Logan said that he'd met Dave before, it was true."

Robin flushed. She didn't want to be singled out in any way. Nor did she want to hear that Al Logan was right about anything.

"I know how you feel about Al," Wolff went on. "But the day we met Dave, the day *before* his second surgery, Dave actually threw something at me, and he cursed both of us, in German. The doctors hadn't yet realized that there was pressure on his brain, that a type of temporary dementia had him believing he'd been captured by Nazis. To us it seemed that he was a terrible anti-Semite."

Robin stared at Wolff, open-mouthed. Once she'd found Dave's annex she didn't think she could ever be surprised again. But, Wolff had just managed to do that.

"I think Dave remembers it, but he can't say anything, because he's always denied these things. Only God knows for sure, but I'm sure certain that's the reason he's kept so many things from you."

Robin was listening intently to Wolff of course, but, at the same time, she wondered what Wolff could have done that had him looking so guilty.

"After Dave cursed me," Wolff said, "I didn't wait to find out if anything was wrong. I stormed out of his room. I was furious. I just thought: how dare this anti-Semite, this Nazi, attack me. I didn't listen. That is a great sin. But, thankfully, before I went home for the Sabbath—it was the same weekend that you came to Sioux Falls, Robin–I went back to his room.

"I was so angry. I thought I was almost finished with that part of my life. But Dave had brought it all back, as strong as ever. If only for that reason – never mind the curses – I might have really hurt Dave. I might even have killed him."

From the far end of the table, Faiga reached out her hand to her husband, as though to comfort him. Then she drew her hand back. The Blumen's did not touch in public, and, clearly, Faiga understood that Wolff needed to say these things, a kind of confession.

Wolff smiled at his wife. Then he stood up, as though that made it easier to speak.

"When I went back to his room, Dave had collapsed. Al Logan was gone. Dave was surrounded by medical staff. They were ignoring what he was saying of course. But I understood. By then he was going on and on in Yiddish, about how they had never been able to kill his mother or father, and that they wouldn't kill him either. Clearly, he thought he was in a concentration camp. Clearly, he intended to survive. I think Dave's whole life has been about that survival."

Beside her, Robin heard Jacob take several deep, sharp breaths, like wounds. Jacob must be crying, Robin thought. But he'd covered his face with his hands, so she couldn't be sure.

Robin reached over to touch Jacob's arm, shooting a look at Wolff, imploring him to stop. But he didn't. Instead he went to stand behind Jacob, putting his hands on the old man's shoulders. Faiga left her place further down the long table to came and take Robin's hand. It was as though the four of them made a strong human chain.

Finally, Jacob took his shielding hands from his tear-stained face, and looked back at Wolff. "Please, go on," he said, his voice carrying such hurt, but also such courage. "I didn't know."

Wolff's smile was tiny, but clearly Jacob's request strengthened him. He kept his grasp on Jacob's shoulders firm and said, "It's just like when I was flying. Sometimes

I'd pretend I was on a bombing run, that I alone would bomb the railroads on the way to the camps, or the crematoria. It was my fantasy, a way to save my parents from the camps, to save the lives of those half brothers and sisters of mine, the children my parents had before the war. For a long time that was my brand of survival. I was still doing it sometime, like when I spotted Dave."

Robin had moved to a place beyond simple surprise. If someone as calm and open as Wolff Blumen had such secrets, then certainly what had happened to his parents could be sufficient reason for Dave to build his annex.

Wolff looked up again; as though to God. "*Hashem* linked Dave and me, I have no doubt. All of this, our meeting, will make it possible for both of us to move on with our lives."

The expression on Jacob's face clearly said that he did not think God had any part in this, but Robin knew he would never debate that with his host. Instead, he answered Wolff with almost glacial calm, "We would have welcomed such bombs, of course. But, you should know that they would have found other ways to kill us, God or no God."

Wolff gave Jacob's thin shoulders a squeeze, looked at Robin in a way that asked forgiveness for the pain he was causing, and said, "I was so upset that I had come to harm Dave that I almost fainted. The doctors told me to go home and pray for this man, that they would look after the medical matters. I've been praying ever since, for Dave and for me, for all of us."

Beside her Jacob was now sitting straight, his face impassive. But he still held her hand tightly and kept repeating, "I didn't know. I didn't know."

✡

Robin wasn't able to tell Dave any of this right away, which was a kind of blessing, since she needed time to digest it herself. Fortunately, she had some lighter subjects she could share with Dave: the fact that Wolff and Faiga had their wish, they would be going back to the East Coast. That seemed to cheer him a little. Other than when he heard that news, Dave was silent and suffering that weekend, just like Jacob.

He knows how his father spends the High Holy Days, Robin thought. That's bothering him almost as much as anything I've said. She would have liked to comfort him, but, when they'd made their plan, Jacob, Wolff, Faiga, and Robin, they had all agreed that Dave's had to be somewhat isolated for their plan to work well. Nothing Robin had learned had changed her mind about going forward with their plan.

She was even willing to tell Sunny an untruth to move the plan forward. "Daddy has a cold," she said when Sunny asked when they were going to see Daddy. "I'll take you to see him the minute he's better."

Sunny, playing cheerfully with the children in the synagogue day care, reminded her, "And then on Wednesday Shayna and I will take him birthday cake and balloons, right?"

Happy birthday parties for little girls seemed very far away.

The day after *Rosh Hashanah,* Monday morning, Robin, Jacob and Wolff met as agreed in Wolff's office. This time Jacob had been adamant. Robin would not confront Dave again without support. Wolff and Jacob would be waiting for her outside his hospital room.

Several times in the last few days Jacob had referred to the duty he had to Sunny and Robin. At lunch the day before he'd repeatedly called Robin, '*tochter*.' Robin had caught the sense of it without asking, but when they'd cleaned up the kitchen together, Faiga had confirmed that *tochter* was Yiddish for 'daughter.' Every time Jacob said it Robin's eyes filled. Had she acquired a father even as she might have lost Dave?

Margarita Razkowski, a small, gentle woman, had arrived in Sioux Falls on Sunday night. She had two suitcases with her, one filled with toys: something for every one of the Blumen children, a doll for Sunny and another for Shayna, one blonde, one brunette. She had brought Robin a gift too, a beautifully-wrapped old-fashioned looking wristwatch. Robin had protested such an extravagant present, but Margarita had said, "No, you must take it and wear it. A watch, to say that we must make up for lost time. Better it would have been a watch from the old country, but that is impossible. But the style is something like the old days. I saw this, so much like what my mother used to wear, when I was shopping for the girls. I knew it was made just for you."

Today Robin's job was to inform Dave that now both his parents were in town and that they insisted on seeing him. Once that had been accomplished Dave would be given their ultimatum: no more secrets, no more dangerous climbing trips. Although Robin would do the talking, the three of them–Wolff, Jacob, and Robin–were the delegation.

They had just reached the fifth floor when they were greeted by Dave's favorite orderly.

"Hi, Robin. Rabbi, did you hear? Al Logan, the ON-The-Spot guy who reported your rescue of Dave, is back in town. He got a new job while he was on vacation, but he said he had to come back to say good-bye. He's going to have a new show on Cable, an expose sort of thing. He's calling it *White Hot*."

Robin froze. She stepped in front of Wolff to question the orderly, not even bothering to excuse herself.

"What exactly did he say?"

"Nothing to concern you; he just talked about the subject of his first show. It's something about secret bunkers built for protection by people who fear the past.

"He played the TV ad for the show. It has clips of the first show. You hear the title – *White Hot* – and this kind of spooky music. You watch; he'll be real famous one day."

Robin barely heard the end of the orderly's enthusiastic description. She was already retreating down the hall to the ward's waiting room. Wolff and Jacob followed, clearly confused by her sudden change of direction and by the look on her face.

Hospital waiting rooms had become very familiar to Robin. This one had been one of her havens. She'd spent enough time there to have a favorite corner. She headed for it now, shrinking down in a corner of the leather sofa as if she hoped the cushions would swallow her up.

The expression on Wolff's face made his concern clear, as did his anxious question. "Robin, are you okay?"

Jacob Razkowski threaded his way more delicately. "What that young man out there said upset you, yes?"

Robin looked up, still unwilling to tell them everything. But secrets now, hers or Dave's, were ridiculous. "You wouldn't realize of course, because there was some stuff I didn't tell you the other night. It was something

I wanted to tell Dave before anyone else knew. I can't even imagine his reaction."

She shuddered.

"That first show of Al Logan's—it's about Dave. Al broke into our house while I was in Minneapolis. After Tovah and I found the annex, Al broke in and got pictures."

"You're sure it was Al?" Wolff said.

Robin's looked at him, witheringly. "Do you think I'd accuse him, if I wasn't sure? Yes, it was Al. He came by the house earlier the same night. He said he wanted to return Dave's things, the stuff he claimed he got from the Ranger. I should have known something was fishy, but I didn't figure it out. Tovah and I had just found the annex. That night I heard noises. I ran upstairs to the entrance in Dave's office. I saw someone, a man. He certainly had a video camera. I saw the light. I almost caught him that night, but I fell."

Wolff sat down beside her.

Robin finished up. No more secrets. "I don't think we can fix this. It's gone too far. Dave will never forgive me for allowing Al Logan to get into the house, into his bunker. It's his biggest secret of all and it will be on national television. Can you just imagine?"

There were quick footsteps in the hall then, before either Wolff or Jacob could respond. The orderly who had just told them about Al's show flashed by the waiting room door. His voice floated back to them: "556A needs help. 556A, stat!"

There was a controlled stampede of footsteps toward the opposite end of the hall. Robin, Wolff, and Jacob recognized the hurried sounds of medical personnel who could move quickly without actually running.

Robin leapt to her feet. "556A! Dave! That's Dave! He's in trouble!"

Then she realized something. "Oh my god; why didn't I think of it before? Dave already knows about Al's show. He always turns on the TV to get the morning news."

The three of them hurried down the hall, Robin in the lead. She'd have liked to run, to catch up with the nurse ahead of them in the hallway, but she didn't want to outpace Jacob. Had Dave somehow injured himself when he heard about Al's show?

There was no other staff visible. The central nurses' station had been deserted. The medication room behind the station stood empty. The metal rolling stand that held patient charts seemed to have been left in charge, a flat-faced robot.

They finally reached Dave's room. The wide door was still swinging. Robin caught it and held it for a moment, wondering if she had the nerve to go further. Of course she did. She had to. She pulled the door open and then stopped in the doorway, blocking Wolff and Jacob.

The small private room had probably never held so many people. All the staff huddled together on the far side of Dave's bed. Even Dave's surgeon, Katherine Haines, was there. One thing was immediately obvious: there was no medical crisis.

No one in the room was paying any attention to Dave. Instead they were all looking up, concentrating on the far corner of the room, near the ceiling.

High above their heads, the wall-mounted television set hung askew. Both the screen and the picture tube had exploded. Broken glass, silvery light and dark, lay scattered on the floor of the room and on the armchair in the corner. There were even shards of glass on Dave's bed.

As Robin watched, Dr. Haines turned away from the shattered set. Working delicately, as though she was performing a new medical procedure, she began to pick pieces of glass off Dave's bed. When she had handful of shards she looked around, apparently searching for a reasonable place to deposit them. With a shrug of her shoulders she dropped them to the floor, where they made a pretty ringing sound as they landed.

Robin had no trouble reconstructing what had happened. The remnants of a red and black Channel 7 KLON coffee mug, a gift from Al Logan, lay on the floor along with the fragments of the television screen and picture tube.

Dr Haines scraped together some of the glass on the floor with the side of her neat brown oxford. Contemplated the mess, she said, in the most conversational tone, "How am I ever going to explain this in committee?"

Mirroring her matter-of-fact tone perfectly, Dave suggested, "Tell them a careless patient had an accident. Tell them he dropped a coffee mug. Tell them he'll pay for it–the television that is, not the mug. In fact, tell them the patient said it'll be a pleasure to pay for it, that it will be worth every damn cent."

Robin could only imagine what the scene would have been had Dave been able to reach the real Al Logan. It might have been the newsman lying on the floor in several pieces instead of a souvenir coffee mug. She would have cheered Dave on in any action he'd taken against Al.

She had moved into the room now, so Wolff stood in the doorway behind her. Dave looked over at Wolff and smiled. "Don't worry, Dr. Haines," he said. "I never throw more than one thing in a session, even when I miss. Right, Rabbi?"

"You remember!" Wolff Blumen said triumphantly. "I knew you remembered."

Jacob had edged in behind Wolff now, barely inside the room, his expression tentative. What would happen if Dave rejected him?

Then, Dave spotted his father. His face contorted as though he wanted to cry. At the same time he flushed, the first color Robin had seen in his face in days. An expression of profound relief passed over his face, followed by a huge grin. He had just realized that his father hadn't given up on him and gone home. "Papa! Is Mom here, too?"

Robin understood the whole march of emotions – a surprise, relief, embarrassment and finally joy, across Dave's face. There had been nothing of that careful neutral look of his. The loss of his last secret had freed Dave, even if he didn't realize it yet.

Robin had never been so proud of Dave. There was no lapse, not one moment, between his surprise at seeing his father, and his welcome. The bond between the two men was still strong. If she hadn't known better, Robin would have thought that Dave had seen his father only a few days ago, instead of not for more than a decade.

"Papa, you'll have to come here. I can't get to you. But I'm the master of the one-armed hug. Isn't that right?" Dave said that last question to Robin.

"Yes, you are, right." Her response was terse, but she only because there were no words adequate to express her joy at this reunion. When Dave enfolded his father with his one working arm, Robin watching, all three of them were crying.

"Baruch Hashem," said Wolff Blumen, falling back on the traditional blessing of God's Name. "I'm going to phone Faiga, and tell her to bring your mother here."

Wolff left the room with Dr. Haines, both of them looking uncommonly pleased.

CHAPTER TWENTY-NINE

Al leaned back in his chair at KLON after delivering the early Monday morning television news. He couldn't do anything wrong these days. The weekend had been perfect. He'd flown to Atlanta Friday afternoon, made the deal on Saturday. The cable vice-president who'd handled most of the negotiations had to miss the meeting.

"It's the High Holy Days," he'd explained on the phone when they spoke the day before Al arrived in Atlanta. Obviously the man had no hint that Al knew what he was talking about. "But the rest of the team will take you through the papers."

"No problem," Al had said. "No problem at all. Enjoy your holiday." He had loved every minute in Atlanta, holiday or no holiday. He'd signed the papers in a magnificent twentieth floor board room overlooking suburban Atlanta. They'd already told him that his new office would be several stories above the board room.

His boss in Sioux Falls hadn't offered a single argument over the time remaining in his contract. He'd actually seemed grateful that Al had stayed in town for almost four years. "Just do me a favor," he'd said. "Go back on air this week to say good bye."

Al was happy to oblige, happy to use KLON to kick off *White Hot* and his new cable association.

There had been that one unavoidable, uncomfortable conversation with Wolff Blumen. And the Rabbi didn't even know he'd broken into Razkowski's house. He didn't know the content of the new show. He'd probably have something to say about that, if he ever knew the whole story.

Al told himself he didn't care what Wolff Blumen said or did. He didn't need to concern himself with Wolff Blumen any longer. His secrets were safe. No matter what, Wolff would never betray a confidence.

CHAPTER THIRTY

On Wednesday afternoon, Dave's room was almost as crowded as it had been just after he'd thrown the coffee mug. But this time it was a very different crowd and mood. Sunny's and Shayna's birthday party had been brought to Dave.

"Daddy, I actually got them for my birthday. They're my grandparents!" Sunny dragged in Margarita and Jacob, one by each hand, as though they were the newest, most exotic toys.

"I don't know where she got such an idea," Jacob said. "She knows us before, not just today. But she thinks the grandparent part is for the birthday. I've never been a birthday present before. It's not a bad thing at all."

Faiga and Wolff had brought birthday cake for the staff and helium-filled balloons to tie to Dave's bed. There were so many balloons that Dave said he wouldn't need to relearn walking. He would just watch the balloons and learn to levitate.

Dave held court, amusing his guests with his version of the events earlier in the week.

"I heard Al Logan do his *schpiel* for his new show, and then there was a sort of shadowy picture, and then–God-damn it, it was a set–made to look like part of our house. Even then I probably realized it wouldn't really be me, that he wouldn't give my name or anything. But, he'd been in my stairway. I hollered something really obscene, and the orderly high-tailed it out of here. He thought that I was suddenly in pain.

"The fact that it was Logan was the topper! There he was, with my absolutely last secret, at least from the rest of the world, and he was going to put it on television. Al Logan, of all people. I knew right away that he wanted me to know." Dave's audience nodded as one. They did know.

Dave grinned at the gratifying reaction. "Then I spotted the coffee mug. It was as though his face was on it. So I guess… I guess I just kind of… Actually his face was on the television at that moment. So, WHAM! It felt great. And then, all of a sudden, I realized I was free, actually free. There were no more secrets."

There was only one moment of formal ceremony at the birthday celebration. Wolff had a report to give and something to present to Dave.

Wolff had met with Al that morning. "He kept saying how everything was 'without prejudice.' I'm surprised he didn't have a lawyer with him," Wolff said.

Fortunately, he could keep his remarks brief. He couldn't say very much without straying into areas that were private. Al Logan seemed guaranteed professional success now, but he certainly hadn't resolved any of the things that had tormented him. When it came to his own family, Al was leaving Sioux Falls with even more problems than he had brought with him.

Wolff couldn't say that to Dave or anyone else. In the area of his personal life, Wolff felt Al Logan was entitled to the same support and protection as Dave.

Wolff had been standing at the end of Dave's bed. Now he walked over to the left side of the bed, pulling a black plastic case out of his sagging jacket pocket as he went.

"I'd told Al I was calling for you, because of course you were upset about the show. He reacted as if you were going to sue him, although I tried to tell him you couldn't be bothered."

Wolff opened the case he'd pulled out of his pocket and offered the video tape inside to Dave. "So, Dave, I guess what I have here is a birthday present for you. It's not your birthday, of course. But we can call it a gift of re-birth, for your new life. This is a big part of what will be appear on TV. Al sent it over after our meeting."

Dave took the tape out of the case and seemed to weigh it in his hand. His audience couldn't help it; as one they looked up to where a new television set had been mounted.

Wolff looked up briefly too, but he kept talking, as though only his very complete explanation would keep Dave from throwing something again.

"At first Al was very anxious when I asked for this tape, even though I told him you just wanted to be prepared for the content. Then, when I said you would sign a release, he couldn't get it to me fast enough. He guarantees that in exchange for your release no one will be able to identify you. He modified the night scenes he took on the way into your house. He also cut out one scene of the rescue helicopter landing at the hospital. The cable people didn't want him to use it, anyway. So, now all that's left is for us to watch this." Wolff reached over and tapped the tape that was now in Dave's hand.

Dave hefted the tape twice, as though weighing it. He even glanced up at the TV set, smiling wickedly all the while. Then, as though cracking an egg, he rapped the video hard against the metal frame of his bed. The black plastic cover gaped open and glossy brown videotape spilled out in curls.

"I wonder if you would burn this for me when you get outside," Dave said as he handed Wolff the wreckage.

It was only after the girls' birthday party that Dave's hospital room, his haven for so many weeks, began to feel as cramped as a prison cell, as uncomfortable as an interrogation chamber.

There had been moments right after he'd revived from his coma when Dave would have happily stayed in that hospital room, even in bed, forever. It meant his secrets were safe, and it meant that Robin would stay beside him. But now his secrets were shattered, and Robin seemed distant.

He tried sharing his new discomfort at being confined with Wolff Blumen and Dr. Haines, but they both took his complaints as a good sign, saying that he must almost be ready to go home.

No wonder he felt trapped, Dave thought. He'd shifted his entire mental landscape too quickly. Robin was spending the days with him again, which meant he spent most of his time trying to talk to her. Even when she wasn't there he was thinking about what he should have said or what he would say.

He hated what he'd done to his parents. It turned out that neither of them had ever understood the intent of his climbing trips. He always thought it was obvious that they were an effort to emulate his father's bravery, and to make his own memorial to those who'd died. Instead, Jacob had seen them as Dave's way of evading the past entirely.

As for Robin, even when he explained why he'd built the annex–that it hadn't been a long-held plan–although she seemed to believe him, his confession didn't magically heal everything between them.

Robin continued to behave as though he had some huge advantage in their relationship. Since she'd discounted his money and the house, he couldn't imagine what that advantage might be. It certainly wasn't physical. It took the efforts of two orderlies and many agonizing minutes just to get him settled in a wheelchair.

He couldn't yet maneuver the wheelchair, so he was stranded wherever the orderlies left him. Throughout their early conversations Robin stayed out of reach, usually leaning against the small room's farthest wall. He knew he'd have to bridge the distance between them with words alone.

Apparently Robin didn't hold him responsible for all their problems. She willingly took some of the blame for how things had developed during their years together.

She should have insisted on much more from him, she said. Her generosity made Dave feel worse.

He'd have given anything just to get her to come closer. But, he didn't feel he could ask. For her part, Robin seemed to need the support of the far wall. After two days Dave tried to make that into a feeble joke: that she couldn't possibly get farther away and still be in the same room. His attempt at humor didn't help.

His words were so faltering. They wouldn't have convinced him of very much either. "When I came to, after I fell, I wanted you there, beside me, so badly. I kept calling your name. Everyone has said that. I remember that too: calling your names over and over again. 'Robin. Sunny.' Doesn't that tell you something?"

Robin leaned closer to answer him, but she didn't move. "It does, yes, it's touching. And I love you for it; that you wanted me to be there. But, Dave, for you to go to such lengths without telling me what those trips were all about. I don't find that touching."

All he could do was acknowledge what she'd said. He knew he'd better keep on talking, even if he was making a mess of it. If he stopped, he'd never know how to get started again. "You know that moment when I saw the story was going to be on TV: it wasn't only that I was pissed because it was Logan. I also knew how bad it had been ever since you'd come back from Minneapolis. Not talking to each other. I knew that was hard." Then he admitted, "I guess I had spent it not talking."

"True." Robin said. "You did. And we've still got lots we need to say to each other to make up for all that silence." But, finally, she had pulled up a chair and sat down closer to him.

Dave almost wept when he recognized that small concession.

"All the time you were away Minneapolis I couldn't rest," he said. "I knew I needed to tell you...tell you things. But, I didn't know if it had to be everything. I assumed some things like the annex had to remain secrets, to keep everyone safe. It was impossible to know what to tell..."

"And what not to tell," Robin said with far more spirit then she'd ever shown before.

"And what not to tell," Dave agreed. "I'm not very proud of that, but it's true. I couldn't work it out. I knew if I opened my mouth it would all pour out. I don't know why the secrets were so important, except that I'd worked so hard on them, and for so long.

"I mean, I get Jess and everyone else to tell you all the things that occupied me for almost twenty years, the security of having enough money, and it turns out to be a big yawn to you. Is that reasonable? Of course not."

As a joke it wasn't any better than his other attempts. Robin didn't look sympathetic or amused. She just said, "Well, try to imagine what it felt like when they told me about all that money, the house, everything. And then things like those locks on the files in your office. I had to think that I was the one you didn't trust. I didn't know what to think. I was very angry, and hurt too."

It was several days before they reached the subject of Al Logan's break-in. Then Dave was freshly enraged. He hadn't realized when the break-in had taken place. "He must have done it right after you left for Sioux Falls," he surmised.

Robin finally recounted the whole story about her first night back in Minneapolis. "I felt so guilty when I realized what had happened," Robin said, as she finished her story.

"What do you have to feel guilty about?" Dave asked.

"I just told you. He broke in the first night I was there. I'd just found the annex with Tovah. We left the bookcase pulled out. I don't know why exactly. Almost as if that would help convince us it was real. You have no idea what a shock it was to find it. I thought that it meant you were a Nazi. It took Tovah, Wolff's stories, and your parents, to teach me otherwise."

Dave thought Robin looked as though she still wasn't totally convinced. Clearly something was still bothering her.

Finally Robin stood up and went to stand directly opposite him in his wheelchair, facing him as though he was a firing squad.

"You don't seem to realize. Al might not–would not–have found your annex if I'd closed it up again. I'm sorry about that. I really am."

How awful to finally understand that she thought he would be angry at her because Al had discovered the annex.

"I can't believe it," he'd sputtered. His raging sense of impotence almost rendered him speechless. "The nerve of that man, what gall. If he had touched you, threatened you, anything, I would have killed him, not just obliterated him electronically."

But his rage didn't serve either of them. In the end, Dave was made articulate by the urgent need for clarity between him and Robin. "That's why you've been afraid to tell me exactly what happened?"

All Robin could do was nod, because she was weeping. Dave's awkward posture, semi-reclining in the wheel chair, was almost more than he could bear. He tried to reach toward her, but perhaps because of her tears she didn't seem to notice his gesture.

"I hate that I made you afraid," I'm sorry. I apologize for that." Through her tears, and still standing squarely facing him, although still at a distance, Robin's only response was a nod.

"We can go on working on understanding all this…. forever, if necessary," Dave continued. Robin nodded again. "Forever," he repeated.

She was still looking down, but she didn't say anything. Nor did she seem to notice his still-extended hand.

Two weeks later Dave was ready to go home. The trip had turned into an adventure, a chartered flight with Wolff Blumen as their pilot. This would be Wolff's last flight in the Midwest. In a few days the whole Blumen family was leaving for New Jersey.

The ambulance drivers lifted Dave on board Wolff's airplane, positioning him carefully in the seat beside the pilot; then storing his wheelchair in the back. Fortunately most of their luggage had been shipped home in Dave's Jeep, so there was plenty of space.

Robin was nervous, but Dave and Wolff seemed to be treating the whole trip as if it was the most normal method of travel. Sunny wasn't worried either. She had declared herself the flight attendant.

"Everyone strapped in?" Wolff asked.

"Yes, sir," Sunny responded.

"Please be sure the passengers all have their seats and tray tables in the upright position," Wolff said, waiting as Sunny pretended to comply.

Then, obviously without thinking about what he was doing, Wolff went through a preflight ritual that neither Robin nor Dave had ever seen before. Wolff constructed his headdress: side curls tucked behind his ears, skullcap centered, his earphones added, the black hat clapped on to hold everything in place. Robin had to stop worrying at that point. Nothing bad could happen with this man as their pilot.

Robin would have given almost everything to know what the men were thinking. Would Dave have his parents in mind? Jacob and Margarita were coming to visit as soon as they were settled in Minneapolis. Dave had promised them, and Robin, that there would be no more solitary climbing trips, no more secrets, no more isolation from family. Would Dave, looking down as they flew over the land, regret any of those promises? Or, would Wolff offer to show them how he'd once set up mock bombing runs over the Black Hills?

But neither man looked down. They had their eyes straight ahead on the horizon.

"It goes on … forever," Dave said happily. He glanced back at Robin, reaching back to her with his left hand.

Robin reached forward and grasped his hand. "It does. It goes on, probably forever," she said.